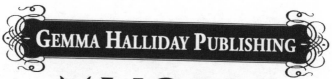
GEMMA HALLIDAY PUBLISHING

MYSTIC MISTLETOE MURDER

A Mystic Isle Mystery
· Book 2 ·

USA Today Bestselling Authors
Sally J. Smith &
Jean Steffens

MYSTIC MISTLETOE MURDER

a Mystic Isle mystery

Sally J. Smith & Jean Steffens

The authors wish to send a shout out to Wendi Baker for overseeing our work on this project, to Sandra Barkevich for her eagle editing eye, and, as always, Janet Holmes for so accurately and beautifully translating our story to cover.

Sally dedicates this Christmas story to Jean Steffens—friend, nurturer, and partner in crime.

And Jean would like to dedicate this Christmas story to Sally J. Smith—friend, advocate, and partner in crime.

~

Please join us for an evening of celebration, entertainment, libation, & gourmet dining.

A *Mystic Mistletoe Merriment Bash*

~December 20~

~6:00 p.m.~

The Mansion at Mystic Isle

Our very special guests will be the young people from St. Antoine's Children's Home, the beneficiaries of our most successful holiday drive ever. And Papa Noël, with his bag of goodies, will be droving his gators on down the bayou to visit us.

Cocktails at 6:00 p.m.

Followed by the dinner stylings of

Chef Valentine Cantrell at 7:00 p.m.

Formal or semiformal attire is requested for this most special evening.

~

CHAPTER ONE

"Ho, ho, ho, y'all. Yat, Miss Melanie Hamilton?" The exaggerated Southern drawl, nothing at all like a real N'awlins accent, came from behind me. The bad accent and sexy voice belonged to resort manager Jack Stockton. It was part of his effort to assimilate and make merry on his first holiday season at The Mansion at Mystic Isle in the heart of the Louisiana bayou. A darn good effort, though not Jack's usual style at all. My guess? He'd indulged in at least a couple of eggnogs and was brimming over with holiday spirit.

I turned around and put my hands on my hips. "Ho, ho, ho, yourself."

Jack walked up to me, visibly swallowing hard. By the way his dark eyes smoked over and his mouth gaped, I could tell the dress and shoes I'd fussed over had the desired effect.

When he found his voice again, what he had to say was just so perfect. "Any man who thinks blondes are it is straight up nuts." His voice had gone soft so others wouldn't hear, and his tone was all husky, giving me shivers. "Redheads rock my world, one in particular, and tonight, in that green dress with her hair like glowing flame, she's more spectacular than a Christmas tree."

Yes, sir. Perfect, just like Cap'n Jack himself—my New York Yankee in King Rex's court, doing his best to understand the New Orleans way of life.

I couldn't suppress a grin but fought off the urge to fall into his arms. Even if I preferred being thought of as a strawberry blonde instead of a redhead, I couldn't remember a more flattering compliment having been directed my way in a while.

We'd been seeing each other several months now, and I was a goner, more stuck on him than Spidey to a skyscraper. If his sweetness and rapt attention were clues, the sentiment was mutual—my Cap'n Jack, which was how I'd thought of him since he arrived and took the position of resort manager.

While I was pretty sure almost everyone at the resort knew we'd been seeing each other, we still tried to keep things cool, platonic, and on the down low in our work environment. Not an easy chore when my handsome boss was around.

I kept my voice soft too. "I was hoping we might track us down some mistletoe later on."

His eyebrows arched, and his grin was wicked. "Stellar idea, Miss Hamilton."

The Mansion at Mystic Isle Mistletoe Merriment Bash was in full swing, and the old dowager queen plantation-turned-resort was all dressed up for the holidays. Four Christmas trees hung with white twinkle lights and gold ribbons anchored the big dining room, while one enormous tree in the center, a near twin to the twenty-foot beauty in The Mansion's main lobby, stood proudly in the middle of the room. Gold and white satin ribbons had been interwoven on the cedar garlands. Christmas was everywhere.

Round tables with gold and white linens had been set with the resort's gold-rimmed holiday china and awaited Chef Valentine Cantrell's traditional four-course réveillon dinner. The aromas coming from the kitchen had been making my mouth water the whole dang night.

Everyone from the invited staff to the invited honored guests also looked very spiffy.

I had taken extra care getting ready for the party. My gorgeous roommate and best friend, Catalina Gabor, the resort's tarot card reader, and I had done each other's makeup and hair, and both had new dresses and shoes purchased just for the occasion of the Christmas party.

I spotted Cat across the room with her beau, Chief Deputy Sheriff of Jefferson Parish Quincy Boudreaux, at her side. Cat had found her dress at Chantelle's Vintage Designs, a secondhand dress shop on Decatur. She was stunning in the cream-colored gown. The sleeveless fitted bodice emphasized her ample bosom, and the flowing gored skirt fluttered when she walked and made her look like some kind of old-time Hollywood goddess.

In comparison, I'd sort of felt like a schoolgirl in my dress. It was a bateau-neck, cap-sleeved cocktail dress with a fitted bodice, belted waist, and full, gathered skirt. The shiny emerald taffeta reminded me of the dress I wore to my high school spring formal. Johnny Mancini, my date, had nearly fallen down when he'd seen me in it. Of course back in high school, I hadn't had the gold-colored leather, four-and-a-half-inch stiletto-heeled sandals to sell my transition to womanhood.

All evening Jack had been looking at me like I was a plum pudding he was ready to sink his teeth into, so I guessed all the trouble I'd gone to had been worth it.

Harry Villars, hotel owner and Southern gentlemen of the grandest ilk, had mingled with all who'd come to the event from the employees to local celebrities. The perfect host, he'd outdone even his usual sartorial grandeur by wearing a Christmas-red suit over a tartan waistcoat and jaunty green bowtie.

"Miss Melanie Hamilton." He walked up to us. "As I live and breathe, aren't you just a vision of loveliness tonight? We are truly blessed here at The Mansion that you agreed to come work for us, grace our halls, and ink your lovely body art for our patrons."

My face went hot. "Why, thank you kindly, Mr. Villars. You're quite lovely yourself."

The former plantation property, now reincarnated as The Mansion at Mystic Isle, had been handed down through the Villars family over almost three centuries. Run-down and ill-used when Harry took it over, he'd spent time and money refurbishing and turning it into a resort for guests who liked to be scared and entertained all at the same time. The motif was *haunted mansion*, and the employees were all purveyors of the paranormal and supernatural. At least that was the hype—every last employee claimed to only be good at playing a role. But the occasional strangeness of things that had happened around the resort sometimes made me wonder.

Tonight's event was the pinnacle of a holiday drive conducted by Harry, Jack Stockton, and me, the official tattoo artiste at Mystic Isle and unofficial New Orleans street artist. The beneficiary of said drive was the orphanage sponsored by St. Antoine's Parish in the Ninth Ward. The church was still struggling years after being decimated by Hurricane Katrina, and whenever I had the chance, I did my best to help out there.

Harry took my hand between his two and patted it. "If you'll excuse me, Miss Hamilton, I'll get this show on the road." He moved away through the crowd to the dais and stood in front of the microphone. His voice carried out over the PA system. "Good evening to all my fine guests tonight, and welcome to The Mansion at Mystic Isle." Harry's accent and languid cadence were a trip backwards through time almost two hundred years. "To those of you who helped make our holiday drive a resounding success, all of us here at the resort would like to say thank you, thank you, thank you. I personally would like to extend my most sincere gratitude to Miss Melanie Hamilton for spearheading this drive..." I blushed as catcalls and shouts of woo-hoo and go, girl circled the room. "And also to Mr. Jack Stockton, for all his devoted labor." Whistles, applause, and a couple of way-to-goes acknowledged the many hours Jack had put in to benefit the children's home. "And to you children from St. Antoine's Parish, I want to let you all know it won't be long now. I, myself, just got word that Papa Noël has been spotted droving through the swamp in his skiff pulled by his eight gators, Gaston, Tiboy, Pierre and Alcee, Ninette, and Suzette. And don't you know Celeste and Renee will be there too. And I hear Papa's bag is plenty full of Christmas goodies for all you children."

Dozens of boys and girls laughed and cheered and clapped, as did all the employees and other guests.

It was enough to warm the heart of old Scrooge himself, and it made all the weeks of everyone's hard work so worth the effort.

"But first—" Harry scrubbed his hands together with glee. "Our very special guests from the St. Antoine's Parish Children's Home and Benjamin Cantrell, son of our own Chef Valentine Cantrell, have a real treat for us." He stepped away from the mic stand and gestured to the group of children who'd lined up behind him.

Benjy Cantrell, the eight-year-old son of my friend and resort head chef, Valentine Cantrell, sidled up onto the dais. He was dressed like a miniature maestro in a holiday tux, his café au lait skin glowing in the reflection of his red plaid Christmas suit. He stood on his toes and slid onto the raised bench in front of the baby grand, placed his small feet on the pedal extender, and nodded to the choral director, Sister Catherine Rose, who looked exceptionally pretty tonight in her long blue gown with her short dark hair tucked behind her ears. She lifted her baton and watched for Benjy's cue. He lifted his hand and began an introduction to "Christmastime is Here." The voices of the children rose sweetly while Benjy played lazy, mellow jazz licks on the ivories. It was purely amazing.

"That kid's some talent, isn't he?" Jack said.

"He is. They say he's a prodigy. He's received an invitation to study at the Childress Music Academy in New Orleans."

Jack whistled. "Wow. That school is just for the very gifted, isn't it?"

"For kids with exceptional talent," I said.

"And—" Valentine's sultry voice came from behind us. "For them kids what's rich, too. I don't even know where to start lookin' for the kind of money they're asking for Benjy to study there. Maybe if I win the Powerball." Her gorgeous hair was normally stuffed under the elasticized cap she wore in the kitchen, but tonight she'd pulled it all back from her face with a sparkly headband only to have it explode out in a celebration of tight braids. Delicate strands of gemstones were woven throughout the braids and sparkled in the golden light from the chandeliers. She was stunning.

Jack lifted her hand to his lips, every bit as gallant as an old-time plantation man himself. Southern ways had a way of rubbing off on people. "You look amazing tonight, Chef Cantrell."

She smiled graciously, a woman comfortable with her own elegance. "You go on, Mr. Stockton." When he released her hand, she leaned over and touched cheeks with me.

"I can't wait for your scrumptious dinner, Valentine," I said. "I have the menu memorized, and I hardly ate a bite all week in anticipation of simply gorging myself tonight."

The song ended, and Harry stepped back up to the mic, still applauding. Sister Catherine Rose led the children off the stage, and Benjy, the cutest little hambone I'd ever seen, took bow after bow after bow.

Valentine held her hands to her cheeks and laughed. "That child was born to be a star." Her voice took on a melancholy note then broke, and she looked at us apologetically. "His daddy would be so proud. 'Scuse me. I better go round up the boy, or he'll just stand there being all Liberace through the whole livelong night."

As she moved away through the crowd, Jack bent to my ear. "What's the story with Valentine's husband?"

"He was killed several years ago, seven years I think, serving in Afghanistan. He'd barely just met their son."

"I didn't know."

"She doesn't speak of it often."

"Sure," he said. "I don't blame her. You'd never get over something like that."

"I guess it's been pretty hard on her, but she's done a great job with her son. He's an amazing kid. I hope she can manage the finances to send him to that school. From what she's told me, it's a heck of a lot of money."

"I can imagine," he said.

Our attention went back to the front of the room as Harry announced, "If you all will find your seats, we'll get the feedbag on." A rustle went through the room as people began to move toward their assigned tables. "Chef Cantrell and her staff have put together a fine menu for us tonight, and while it's a little early in the evening for a réveillon dinner, we're gonna all enjoy the heck out of it anyway."

"Well," I said, turning to Jack. "I guess I'll see you later."

He smiled down at me and laid one hand on my bare arm. His touch was always tender and made me feel—oh, yes I did say it—cherished. "I'm sorry about the table assignments," he said. "Harry just thought it would be advantageous for me to sit at the head table with him and a few of the VIP donors."

"I know. I get it." And I did. Well, sort of. Who wouldn't have wanted to sit next to her best beau at the company Christmas bash? I certainly did, but there was only so much room at the head table, and Harry had it in mind to kill a whole flock of birds with one stone, so to speak, by celebrating the holidays, promoting the resort, and recognizing the generosity of those who'd made big donations to the drive. Not only wasn't there room at the head table for me, but Harry's own life partner, the Great Fabrizio, was dining at a different table. Namely the same as mine.

I found lucky table six right away and took a seat. There was a woman with a really big, eighties-style beehive that was red and green all over like a bowl of Christmas Jell-O had exploded on her head. Her earrings were big flashing snowflakes. The strapless dress she wore was shiny red—and I'd never kid about a thing like this—spandex that barely contained her breasts.

I was certain I'd have remembered if I'd ever met her before, so I offered my hand. "Hello, I'm Melanie Hamilton."

She batted green-mascaraed lashes and smiled. "Barbie," she said. *Not really?* Then in the way of explanation, she offered, "I'm with Aaron. He'll be along now any minute."

I didn't know who Aaron was either, so I just nodded and took a chair.

Cat and Quincy came to the table. Quincy, newly promoted to the rank of Chief Deputy, held the chair for her. I had to admit I was a little jealous she got to enjoy the party with her man. She gave me a quick *who-dat?* look when she had a gander at Barbie. I shrugged.

"Just look at you, chère," Quincy said as he bent down and gave me a peck on the cheek. "Why ain't you jes' hotter than a sriracha-boiled crawfish tonight?"

I wrinkled my nose. "Crawfish, Quincy?"

"Oh, leave her alone, Q." Cat patted my hand. "You know by now to ignore half of what this man says and forget the rest. Right?"

"I do," I said.

Quincy fisted his hand and laid it against his heart. "Ugh," he groaned. "Wounded. Mortally wounded."

When God made the irritating yet not-without-a-certain-charm Quincy Boudreaux, he must have also had it in mind to make Catalina Gabor to temper the crime-fighting Cajun. Like Adam and Eve, they were created to be together despite the volatile nature of their romance. The friction in their relationship only served to ignite sparks between them that went to white-hot flames faster than you could blink an eye. At about five-nine, he wasn't all that much taller than Cat, but he was muscular and put together well. To counterbalance his hair that always seemed to be standing straight up, he had those big ol' brown eyes that could launch missiles depending on his mood.

Cat was built like a brick house, with long, lush dark hair, flashing dark eyes, and a nature as unpredictable as a tempest but as loyal as a Saints fan. I loved her like a sister.

She took hold of Quincy's hand and smiled at Barbie. "Sit down, Deputy, and entertain us with tales of your outrageous adventures and daring exploits chasing villains and thwarting crime in Jefferson Parish."

He laid his hand on hers. "Why, chère, I'd be delighted. You know how I love to impress all you ladies."

And regale us he did.

After about twenty or so minutes of cocktails and conversation, another woman I'd never met approached the table and took an empty chair opposite me. She was a couple of inches taller than my five-three and on the stocky side. Her hair was mud brown like the swirling currents of the Mississippi and straighter than the Causeway Bridge. I'd have guessed she was in her early forties—no makeup, dressed in a conservative long black dress with a matching knit jacket over it. I believed I'd once seen my Grandmama Ida wear one like it to a funeral.

The latecomer seemed to have been rushing to get here on time. Her cheeks were ruddy, hair flat against her head and damp, presumably from the sweat shining on her face. Her expression was grim.

"Hello." Cat put out her hand. "I'm Catalina Gabor." She went around the table. "This is my man, Quincy Boudreaux. Mel Hamilton. And Barbie..." Her voice trailed off.

There the Christmas woman went with the batting of the green lashes followed by, "It's just Barbie."

The newcomer looked from one to the next as roll was called, nodding. When the table grew quiet and no response came, I prodded. "And you are...?"

"Oh," she said. "Diane Conner. My husband is Phil Conner." Her words carried the lilt of the deep South, combined with a touch of backwoods redneck. A lift at the end of her sentences turned them into semiquestions not statements, also typical of certain Southern ladies who were taught never to be presumptuous.

Cat and Quincy turned to me at the same time. "Slim," I said by way of explanation. "You know Slim Conner. He tends bar in the Presto-Change-o Room. Slim's our Papa Noël tonight."

"Oh, right." Cat smiled and turned to Diane. "I just love your husband. He's always so funny and sweet, and such a—" She stopped dead at the glare from Diane's oddly colorless eyes.

Quincy had obviously noticed the animosity too. He cleared his throat. "Awright then."

The Great Fabrizio, the resort's medium and a good friend of mine, walked up behind me, bent, and put his arm around my shoulders. "Good evening, my dear Melanie." His cultured English accent always made my name sound so refined. "How lovely you look this evening. You too, Miss Gabor." With his long silvery hair, he looked a lot like my late Granddaddy Joe who helped raise me. Because of that and because he was a really nice man and kind to me, I had a most peculiar bond with Fabrizio. He took the empty chair next to mine.

Next to come to the dinner table was Stella—Stella by Starlight, the resort's astrologer. At seventy-two Stella was one of the older employees at The Mansion, but she knew just about everything there was to know about divining by the stars. I especially loved her ready smile and soft laughter. While I didn't know much about her past, I always pictured her barefoot with flowers in her hair, holding hands, and dancing Ring-Around-the-Rosie in a San Francisco park to the tune of a Herman's Hermits song.

"Oh, just look at this..." she exclaimed, walking up to the table, "...beautiful room and all these beautiful people. Groovy, baby." She sat in the chair beside Quincy's. "Why, Quincy Boudreaux, as I live and breathe. Do you know you're just about the hottest deputy sheriff on the face of the planet, young man?" Maybe I forgot to mention that in addition to everything else, Stella was an outrageous flirt.

We all chatted and exchanged niceties until a wine waiter in a white brocade waistcoat with matching bowtie walked up to the table offering either a white or red from nearby Pontchartrain Vineyards.

"Are you expecting others?" he asked, indicating the three empty chairs on the opposite side of the table from me.

"They are expecting one other—me." The voice was deep, kind of sexy, the accent hard to pin down. I looked up to see a tall, good-looking dude with broad shoulders and a narrow waist—not that I noticed of course. He was dressed differently than most of the other men who wore dark suits or tuxedos. His choice was a Christmas-green shirt with a black satin gambler's vest, black tie, and black slacks. Barbie looked up and began to—for want of a better word—drool.

"Name's Aaron Bronson." The man had black hair and piercing blue eyes, striking and suave and even looking a little dangerous in his dinner duds. He came around the table, and one by one lifted our hands and pressed his lips against them. It was a genteel Southern gesture, but I didn't have the impression I was looking at a man of the South.

When his lips found the top of Diane Conner's hand, she turned furiously red and ducked her head.

"I work with Chef Cantrell," Aaron added, "in the kitchen."

Diane made a noise that sounded like a horse snorting and yanked her hand away.

Whatever the problem was with Diane, it wasn't a problem with Stella who had her hand up, ready, and waiting when he moved on to her.

Aaron clapped Quincy on the shoulder and moved on to Cat, whose mouth turned up on one side in amusement at such goings on. When he came to me and his warm lips touched my skin, I felt myself blush, somewhat flustered. It was flattering to say the least, oh, sister, the very least.

Aaron shook Fabrizio's hand then rounded the table, took hold of the floozy's hand, and held it out with just the tips of his fingers as if he were presenting royalty. "This lady is Miss Barbara Smith."

While Barbie simpered and scooted around on her chair, Aaron Bronson sat down and signaled the wine waiter to fill his glass with red. He then raised his glass. "To the holidays, ladies and gents," he said. "Merry and bright."

"Merry and bright." The rest of us all chimed in.

Aaron picked up his napkin as waiters began to appear in the dining room with the first course. "I apologize for being late," he said. "I was called to the kitchen for a last-minute detail. Valentine and her son had to leave, so she won't be here for dinner."

"Oh, no," I said. "What a shame. She put together such a wonderful menu for tonight, and now she doesn't even get to enjoy it?"

Diane stage-whispered, "Well, if y'all ask me, that's no loss." I looked up at her in surprise.

She may have meant to say it to herself, but we'd all heard her.

Aaron said, "I agree, Miss Hamilton. It's a real shame we won't have the pleasure of her company tonight." He looked again at Diane as if waiting for further remarks. When none came, he said, "She wished us *all* a real nice evening."

I thought about asking why she had to leave but changed my mind when the appetizer was set in front of me. I'd gone with the shrimp remoulade over the deviled eggs and savory beignet, and one bite made me revel in my choice. How Harry Villars had ever managed to entice the celebrated Valentine Cantrell to The Mansion was a mystery, but there'd been rumors it was mostly because she'd wanted to raise Benjy in the nearby town of Estelle where good schools and a low crime rate drew many families from across the river.

As far as chefs went, Val was a goddess, and her talent drew a clientele to The Mansion separate from those who came to have their fortunes told by Catalina Gabor, or their fantasy image inked onto their skin by me, or their dear departed loved ones contacted by the Great Fabrizio. People from across the Big Muddy and all the way from Baton Rouge would make the trek just to dine at The Mansion.

"So there are two people who won't be joining us?" Diane dabbed at her mouth with her napkin.

"Looks that way," I said.

She lifted her hand and signaled one of the waiters standing off to the side with his hands folded behind his back like a proper butler back in the old plantation days. "Two of these people are not coming," she said briskly, definitely not a question here. "I'll have their appetizers, please, sir?"

I looked down at her empty plate.

Aaron laughed. It wasn't mean or anything, just a laugh. "I'll be sure and tell Chef Cantrell at least her food was a big hit with you, Mrs. Conner," he said.

Quincy applauded. "Awright then."

CHAPTER TWO

———

The main course dishes were being cleared—the menu had offered our choice of prime rib with porcinis au jus, poached lobster tails with lemon butter sauce, or duck a l'orange. Oh my sweet goodness. I'd wanted all three, but settled on lobster tails. Heaven.

Harry came around to our table.

"Mrs. Conner," he said. "How nice to see you here."

Diane Conner smiled tightly.

Harry went on. "I was wondering if by chance you might have heard from your husband."

She didn't answer right away, and Harry looked a little confused before he said, "You did know he—" He lowered his voice to just above a whisper. "—agreed to play Papa Noël for us tonight. You know, for the children, and I'd hoped to hear from him by now. They'll be serving dessert and coffee up real soon."

I was beginning to wonder if she was going to give him the courtesy of a reply when she finally shook her head. "No. I haven't heard from him since early this afternoon. But I'm not at all surprised. If you wanted someone reliable, Mr. Villars, you shouldn't have asked my no account husband. He's a true scalawag that man, the kind who'd hightail it out of town with all the Christmas loot."

Harry put his fingertips against his lips and uttered a soft, "Oh, dear me," before turning away and heading back to the main table where he sat down and said something to Jack.

It was then that coffee and our choice of Valentine's luscious desserts were served. Diane Conner once again asked for any leftovers. "I had a hellacious day, and so far the evening's even worse," she explained at the looks of astonishment around her.

That was when the real party started. Harry had hired two little men to act as Papa Noël's elves for the evening. Their job was to circulate around the room, singing Christmas favorites while handing out traditional holiday goodies to the kids from the children's home.

The outfits the *elves* were to wear consisted of a long-sleeved red and white striped T-shirt, red knee pants with green suspenders, bright green leggings, red pointy-toed elf shoes, and a red and green jester's hat with a jingle bell at the tip of it. The perfect costume to endear the elves to the children—I thought so anyway.

The only problem was that one of the little people had left yesterday for Hollywood to audition for a remake of *The Wizard of Oz*, leaving us shy one Christmas elf. Jack had said no one could be found to substitute, no one quite as suitable anyway.

The resort's morose bellman, whom we'd nicknamed Lurch, had stepped forward and offered to stand in. Over seven feet tall and half that in breadth, Lurch as one of Papa Noël's Christmas elves wasn't exactly what you would have called typecasting. But he was game, and no one else wanted to do it, so...

As the DJ put on a background of one of the Christmas songs, a rich, awesome baritone belted out the lyrics to "Christmas in New Orleans," and the French doors to the main dining room opened. Lurch ducked his head and made a grand entrance. The red and green jester's hat was perched on top of his head like a party favor. The striped T-shirt was stretched so tight across his broad shoulders and chest I worried it would turn to shreds any second like the Incredible Hulk's clothes always did. The pants were made to be really baggy, so that wasn't as much of a problem, but they were also made for someone three and a half or four feet tall. So the elf pants on a dude Lurch's size were more like Daisy Dukes. It looked as if someone had managed to find a pair of bright green tights the size of a small circus tent so at least his legs were covered. Obviously the tiny pointy-toed elf shoes wouldn't have worked. Instead his feet were covered in a pair of bright green Converse high-tops, size sixteen or seventeen unless I missed my guess.

Lurch strode in and stopped just inside the doors to let the full effect of his appearance impact the crowd. He began to do-si-do in time to the music, and it became clear it wasn't Lurch's voice whose melodic tones filled the dining room. The singer was the remaining small person who hadn't deserted his post to chase down Hollywood dreams. It was he giving us that great rendition of the Christmas song made famous by Louis Armstrong. And he was doing it while standing on top of Lurch's shuffling feet, one arm wrapped around Lurch's knee, the other clutching a cordless mic. Lurch held his cell phone in one hand and appeared to be snapping off pictures of the room, the crowd, and even some of the smaller elf.

Cat and I exchanged a look of amused surprise.

Stella couldn't seem able to take her eyes off Lurch. "Oh, my, would you look at those legs," and began to fan herself with a copy of the menu that had been left by each dinner plate. "Outta sight."

Cat and I looked at each other and began to clap our hands in time to the music. Diane Conner stared openmouthed.

"Brilliant," Fabrizio said with enthusiasm. "Good show."

Aaron and Barbie joined Cat and me in clapping, and Quincy began to sing along.

The section of the room where the children were seated came to life with squeals of delight as the bizarre ballet proceeded.

All in all, the adorable singing elf and the colossal dancing *elf* were a huge hit.

They'd just finished their first number and were circulating among the children with candy canes and child-sized Santa hats when Jack stepped up to the podium. "Ladies and gentlemen, we're still expecting a special visit from Papa Noël. Papa's running a little late, but he should be here any—"

The double doors were thrust open yet again, and Odeo Fournet, the resort grounds keeper, came running in, the whites of his eyes enormous in his dark face. He looked truly terrified, as he stopped in the middle of the room and blurted, "Oh. My. Goodness. He dead. He dead."

Everyone stared at Odeo, who looked so upset he could barely stay upright. With a look of dismay, Jack stepped down off the stage and started for him but wasn't in time to keep Odeo from crying out, "It's Papa Noël. He dead. Oh, Lord. Like that song, Papa—he got run over by a reindeer."

Silence took over the room, and then a low keening rumble began like wind building up before a hurricane as Lurch moaned. The children began to cry. Chattering. Whispering.

Odeo, sweet, emotional man who he was, began sobbing just as Jack reached him, put his arm around Odeo's shoulders, and began to lead him back out. Jack lifted his chin in an obvious sign to Quincy, who got up from the table and met the two men at the entrance.

Harry went to the mic. "Ladies and gentlemen, it would appear there might have been a mishap. I'm asking you all to remain seated until we figure out just what's happened."

Cat and I, of like mind, stood at the same time and headed for the doors, following Jack, Odeo, and Quincy out of the dining room wing and into the lobby.

The band working the Presto-Change-o Room was grooving to a Zydeco version of "Rockin' Around the Christmas Tree," and the resort guests celebrating in the bar and restaurant were laughing, talking, and dancing. Just like any other holiday evening, just like no one had run in and announced someone had died.

As we crossed the threshold, the signature funeral dirge that played whenever someone went in or out foretold a dark end to the gala evening. Out front on the big veranda, Cat and I hung back as Quincy took Odeo aside. The night air was cold and damp, and both of us shivered in our lightweight party dresses.

"Odeo," Quincy's voice was steady, even, but not unkind. "Come on here, Odeo. Get hold o' yourself. Tell me what you saw."

Stammering, stuttering, Odeo finally managed, "It's Slim. He dressed up like Papa Christmas. In the red suit and all, and he lyin' in the mud with tracks running all up and down him."

Quincy gave Jack a hard look and said, "Well then, you better be showing me."

Odeo began to shake. "No, sir, Deputy, I don't want to go back dere."

"Now, Odeo, you got to show us where he's lying."

Jack put his hand on Odeo's big arm. "I know it's hard, Odeo, but we have to take care of him. Slim's one of ours. If he's hurt—"

"Oh, he ain't hurt," Odeo objected. "He dead. Real dead, Mr. Stockton."

"Lead us to him, then," Jack said. He looked back and saw Cat and me standing in the doorway and shook his head at me as he stepped off the veranda with Quincy and Odeo. The three men headed out across the driveway, over the lawn, and toward the lake, Odeo stumbling a little but leading the other two.

Cat looked at me. "Jack wanted us to stay here."

I nodded. "I know."

We waited a couple of beats before stepping off the veranda together and following the men.

Out along the service road, the three men stopped. It was dark out there, but a couple of pole lights along the road cast a hazy glow on the ground.

It had rained hard the day before, and the gravel service road hadn't held up well under the downpour, disintegrating into a muddy mess. Cat and I stayed on the grass to keep from ruining our party shoes, but we could see well enough what had sent Odeo into near hysterics.

A plump man in a plush Santa suit lay facedown in the mud. And, yes, there were tracks in several places across his back, but not reindeer tracks as Odeo had said, tire tracks, and there were a lot of them like someone had taken more than one good run at the poor soul.

He was unmoving. Dead, I figured, just like Odeo thought. I didn't want to get any closer. Cat seemed to be satisfied where she was too.

Quincy, mindless of his tux, hunkered down in the mud. He laid a hand on the body near the neck then reached for his cell. His voice carried across the night. "It's Chief Deputy Quincy Boudreaux. We got us a body out at The Mansion at Mystic Isle. Gonna need a wagon and some backup."

I was chilled to the bone, and not just because the December wind blew right through me. Slim had been a nice man. He'd worked at The Mansion for a couple of years, tending bar in the Presto-Change-o Room. Everyone liked him. And now he was dead.

Movement caught my eye, and I turned my head to see Diane Conner standing off to one side. I nudged Cat.

"Oh, no," Cat said.

"She shouldn't be out here," I said.

We both turned at once and walked up to Diane. She stared at the crumpled red heap in the middle of the service road. Her face was implacable. Her eyes dry. I tried to turn her away, but she jerked back and kept looking. "Is that him? Is that my husband?"

"Shh, now," Cat soothed. "Come back inside, Mrs. Conner."

I took Diane's other arm, and we led her back toward the resort. "You don't need to be out here now."

A light rain began to fall just as we mounted the veranda. I'd been involved in a murder investigation before, and as sad as I was to know that Slim had bitten the dust, I couldn't help but think *Rain. There goes the crime scene.*

CHAPTER THREE

———

The area near the front entrance was crowded. The low buzzing and murmuring throughout the open lobby testified to the curiosity of all the Looky Lous.

Catalina led Diane through the crowd and the front entrance. She steered Diane into the main salon where the lights were low for cocktails and hors d'oeuvres and light supper service since the main dining room had been closed for the banquet. Diane could sit down in there and not be bothered by all the hullabaloo sure to go on once the place was overrun with the sheriff's people. I watched as my friend and the newly widowed woman went into the salon, wondering at Diane's stoical demeanor at the discovery of her husband's dead body.

As I stepped over the threshold, the funeral dirge sounded again. With everyone coming and going, that would get old pretty fast. Lurch and his Mini-Me met me just inside the door. Lurch spread his arms, palms up, asking in his inimitable way if there was anything he needed to do.

I nodded, keeping my voice low. "It's Slim Conner. From the looks of it, someone ran him down. I'm pretty sure the deputies are going to want folks to hang around here. So if Harry says it's okay, you might want to encourage people to stay inside."

Lurch nodded, and as I approached the salon, the Great Fabrizio rushed up. "Harry's trying to keep things status quo in the dining room," Fabrizio said. "He dispatched me to learn what is happening."

"It's Slim," I said. "Dead."

"Oh, dear me," Fabrizio's brows came together, and his mouth drew tight, his gentle nature rejecting such violence. "I'll go straightaway and explain to Harry."

"Quincy called the sheriff's office for an investigative team," I said, my voice still soft and low.

Fabrizio's hand shook as he raised it to his forehead. "Please send someone for Harry when the authorities arrive," he said.

The dirge rolled again as Jack came through the entrance. "Lurch," he called. "Let's see if we can't get the sensor to stop playing the blasted song for the time being."

Lurch moaned and went to adjust the motion detector mounted on the wall by the front entrance.

Fabrizio went straight to Jack, who gave me a look I thought was intended as comfort and support. What I really needed for comfort was Jack to be with me, but he'd have so much to handle with what had happened, the best thing I could do to help him would be to leave him alone unless he needed me for something.

I waited in the main salon with Cat and the Conner woman. Diane was seated on one of the antebellum-style loveseats, sipping a glass of brandy and staring at the floral pattern in the circular rug that defined the seating space. Cat and I were way more ants-in-our-pants than she was. Shock, maybe?

After a while Jack came in with Quincy and Harry Villars. Quincy took hold of Diane's hand. His voice, usually so teasing and confident, was somber. "Missus Conner, I'm ever so sorry to have to break it to you, but your husband, he's dead."

She looked up at him, and now there was regret both on her face and in her voice. "I was outside earlier. I saw his...his..."

Quincy nodded and patted her hand. "I'm so sorry," he said again. "From all appearances it was a hit-and-run. Terrible shame." His eyes found Cat's first, then mine, in a clear message to keep our mouths shut and let him speak. "One of the things that's also bothering us is that Papa Noël's bag seems to have disappeared. It was loaded with cash and goodies after all."

Diane didn't speak.

Quincy went on. "I don't suppose you'd know if he'd told anyone his schedule, if anyone would be knowing what time to expect him to arrive?"

She squinted at him. "You said 'hit-and-run,' didn't you, Deputy Boudreaux? A hit-and-run is a pure accident. Why're you asking about who knew when he was coming?" She considered him with flat grey eyes, and then a light came into them. "You don't think this was an accident, do you? Y'all are thinking he was run over intentionally, and the Christmas bag was stolen?"

Quincy swallowed. "Yes'm. We do."

Cat took in a breath as I let one out—both audible. "Oh, Q," Cat said. "No. He was murdered?"

"Yes, chère, we're pretty sure somebody run him down and took all his Christmas goodies."

It was Jack's turn to speak. "The resort would like to extend our deepest sympathies to you, Mrs. Conner. If there's anything we can do—"

She drained the snifter and held it out. "You can see that these keep coming to me for at least a little while, until I get used to being a grievin' widow," Diane said. She turned back to Quincy. "If you're sniffing around for a place to start, Deputy, I highly recommend you take a close look at the cook."

"Cook?" Quincy said.

"Cantrell, the cook?" she said.

Harry drew back. "Chef Valentine Cantrell? Why would the sheriff want to look at Chef Cantrell?"

Diane threw up her hands. "I have never been one to cast aspersions, but I'm just sayin'. That woman is where you want to start your investigation. I believe you will find she had good reason to be angry at my husband. She was in love with him, head over heels, and he up and just dumped her. And if anyone needs money, I hear it's that Miss Valentine Cantrell. Her boy needs it to go to school, you know. She might not have been above killing her lover to get his booty." For once she didn't lift her voice at the end, making what was tantamount to an accusation against my friend a declaration. "I mean, land o' mercy, y'all."

We all looked around at each other, but it was pretty clear Diane was finished speaking. She'd sat back in the love seat and lifted a lace hankie, dabbing at her forehead just like a belle of the deep South from days gone by.

"You don't say." Quincy watched Diane who now seemed to be suffering from an old-fashioned case of the vapors. "Well, fiddledeedee."

Harry cleared his throat. "Is there anyone we can call for you, Mrs. Conner? Someone who might come and help take care of you? Get you home?"

Diane shook her head. "There was just my husband, and now he's gone." She looked up at Harry. "I don't want to go home. It will be ever so lonely."

Harry's eyes were moist, his chin quivering. "I totally understand, dear lady. I'll see to it that you have accommodations for tonight. You don't need to be all alone at home in an empty house."

She looked up at him with what appeared to be gratitude.

"Do you have any further questions for Mrs. Conner?" Harry asked.

Quincy shook his head. "Not just now, but…"

"I know, Deputy," Diane said. "I watch TV. How do they say it? 'Don't leave town?'"

"Yes'm," Quincy said.

Excusing himself, Harry led Diane from the room just as Jack came back with a new brandy snifter. "Harry said that bag held everything collected for the children's home," Jack said, tossing the brandy down his own throat and growling at the burn.

"Everything?" My stomach sank then turned over as I remembered… "The cash donations for Nicole weren't in that bag, were they?" When I saw the way his face fell, I knew. "Oh, no."

Jack nodded. "There was over $70,000.00 in cold hard cash in a separate envelope earmarked for Nicole's bone marrow transplant. It's gone, along with all the toys and gift cards donated for the other children from the children's home." He hung his head. "All gone."

My heart sank so low, I thought for a minute it might have stopped beating. One of the children from the home, a ten-year-old named Nicole, was losing her battle with leukemia. A bone marrow transplant was her only option, and it broke my heart to think that sweet child, who only wanted to hang out with her pals and lip-synch Ariana Grande tunes, might not be able to have the procedure because some low-life killer thought he needed the money more than she did.

"That beautiful little girl—she's been through so much already." Nicole's face swam before my eyes, with her big waif-like eyes, the colorful bandanas she wore over her balding scalp. "Whoever did this," I said, feeling righteous anger boiling up, "is a soulless demon. Kill a good man like Slim, and steal from sick and needy children?"

"We're gonna jump right on to catching him, chère," Quincy said.

"You bet your boots you will," I said. "And if you don't, I can think of a lot of people who will."

Cat and I went back into the lobby with Jack and Quincy.

"I guess I better head back to the dining room and run damage control," Jack said. "You going to be okay?" He asked me, concern clouding his warm, brandy-colored eyes.

I nodded.

It was still misting, so as we stepped across the threshold, Lurch grunted and handed me an umbrella.

"Thanks," I said, noticing he'd at least removed the jester's hat but was still wearing the makeshift elf costume. His cohort, the little man with the great singing voice, came up beside us and took hold of Cat's hand. "Let me escort you, beautiful. Wouldn't want you to slip and fall down on that gorgeous keister now. Would we?"

Cat just looked at him, amusement in her eyes. "I don't think we've been formally introduced."

Sweeping one arm in front, he bowed, the bells on the toes of his elf shoes jingling merrily. "Marvin Pendleton, and you are?"

"Catalina Gabor," she said simply.

"I'm delighted," he said.

"And I'm spoken for," she said, as Quincy stepped up and glared down at the gallant Christmas elf.

Marvin looked up at Cat with regret. "My loss, Miss Gabor. I'm now officially devastated."

"You and the rest of the men in Loo-siana." Quincy took Cat's hand and hooked it around his elbow. "You and Mel stay here, darlin'. Those high heels are too pretty to ruin in all that mud, and I'm still hoping you can wear them when you model that new black lacey thing I bought you."

"Whatever you say, Q." She smiled and nodded as he opened his umbrella, stepped off the veranda, and headed back out to where a big tent had been set up over the body.

I looked at her as I opened the umbrella. "Coming?"

"What do you think?" she said as she fell in beside me under my umbrella, and we ventured out into the misty night together.

CHAPTER FOUR

———

It was around eight thirty, cold, wet, dark. A typical bayou December night, except there was a dead body lying in the mud in the middle of the service road that ran from the boathouse area around to the back of the property. The road was used for delivery access to the kitchen and other areas of the resort.

Cat and I stood shivering just outside the crime scene tape under the edge of the tarp where we were out of the rain. My gold high-heeled sandals were probably ruined, but I didn't care. I couldn't stop staring at the white plastic tarp covering what had been my friend and co-worker, Phillip "Slim" Conner.

Slim had been the perfect bartender for The Mansion at Mystic Isle. He knew more jokes about ghosts and magicians and purveyors of the supernatural than I ever knew existed. He had a story for every occasion and a big wide grin that went along in the telling of them. His beard stayed with him year-round, as did his girth. The wizard's robe and pointed hat he wore behind the bar in the Presto-Change-o Room made him look like Dumbledore. And although I hadn't given it much thought until now, he was also the living embodiment of Papa Noël. *He had a broad face, and a little round belly that shook when he laughed, like a bowl full of jelly.*

I would miss him.

Cat was quiet, and I knew she was feeling the same way I was.

Several pole lights that had been set up under the tent cast long shadows but otherwise provided great light for the forensics team from New Orleans to work by. Jefferson Parrish was too small for its own forensics team or medical examiner.

Both had been available to cross the river from New Orleans and be there for Papa Noël.

It was a sad and depressing scene. Uniformed deputies and plain clothes personnel measured and took photos of what the rain had left of the tire tracks.

Quincy, looking handsome and nothing like a working sheriff's chief deputy in his tux, stopped beside one of the forensics officers. "If we got the staff, let's post one of our boys out here overnight so nothing changes until we can get a really good look at the ground when it's dried up. That way we can get us some casts done and get a bead on dem tires."

He looked up and saw us standing there and came over, took off his jacket, and put it around Cat's shoulders. "I'm pretty sure I say, 'Stay inside, darlin'.'"

Cat nodded and smiled, just the corners of her mouth turning up. "That's right. You did."

He looked at her, amused. "Just checking, my sweet." He turned to me. "And you. Are you thinking you goin' be playing at investigator again?"

I shrugged. "Only if you guys don't do your job."

"We're doin' it. Ain't we?"

"So far," I said.

"Well, awright then." He took hold of Cat's arm in one hand, mine in the other, and guided us back around to face the main building. "We just 'bout done here for the night, you see. So..."

Cat and I took the hint and started back for the main building just as an ambulance pulled up beside the crime scene. They'd be loading the body—med examiner.

"What a night," Cat said as we squished through the soggy lawn. "This didn't turn out anything like I expected tonight."

"I know. What a shame. And not just for Slim. There were others who lost out tonight." I shivered.

Cat hooked arms with me and leaned in, giving me the warmth of her body. "I know."

As we took the stairs up onto the veranda, the resort shuttle pulled up under the portico. The orphans from the children's home swarmed over both the lobby and the Christmas elves. Lurch went from child to child, bending low so the selfies he kept snapping off included both his face above and each child's below—like some kind of bizarre totem pole.

The shuttle driver beeped the horn, opened the door, and stepped out onto the asphalt. The resort shuttle bus was similar to an airport shuttle only N'awlins style and couldn't have been more perfect for transporting orphaned children. The front end was a purple Mardi Gras mask with headlights serving as eyes. On either side, The Mansion at Mystic Isle was scrolled in gold letters over dark but beautifully screened images glimpsing into the paranormal world of spirits and spells. It carried guests and employees back and forth from the ferry dock via Jefferson Parish into the swamplands near the Barataria Preserve then over the bridge to the privately owned four square miles of swampland that was now the country's first, and possibly only, resort catering to those who believed in all things mystical and occult.

Sister Catherine Rose and two other nuns shooed the distraught children from the lobby out to the veranda then onto the bus. Sister Catherine stopped beside me. "That poor, poor man," she said.

I nodded. "It's a terrible thing, Sister."

Her tone was reverent. "I'll say a prayer tonight for his soul—"

I spoke before she finished. "And say one for the children too, especially Nicole. Papa Noël's bag was stolen. It had everything in it for the children's Christmas and Nicole's procedure. It's all gone."

Her expression was calm but concerned. "A great loss as well."

"But we'll get it back," I said, and while I wasn't sure how we'd do it, I meant every word.

"What's been going on in there?" Cat asked.

The nun shrugged. "Not much. We all knew something was going on out here, and Mr. Villars, Mr. Stockton, and a few officers came around to all the tables while we were all still in the dining room to take our names and say there was a police matter being investigated and that we all might be contacted in that regard, you know."

I looked up as Jack walked out onto the veranda, handing Cat and me each a blanket before going over to have a word with the shuttle driver. When he came back, he said, "Sister, I've made arrangements for you to take the public ferry. Our shuttle can cross over on it too then take you and the kids straight back to St. Antoine's. The less stress on you and the children, the better."

The bus loaded up, and as it pulled out, heading for the main road, I asked Jack, "What's been going on in there?"

He shrugged. "Not much. We've just been making a list."

I looked up into his big brown eyes. "And checking it twice?"

He didn't react, and I realized I was making a joke when someone had died.

Sobering thought to say the least.

It was a little after nine by that time. The adrenaline rush had left me cold and exhausted, and I yawned and sat down in one of the white wicker fanback chairs. The rain hadn't blown in, and the seat was dry, but I was so drained I wouldn't have cared if it hadn't been. Cat sat in the one beside me.

Jack reached down and took hold of my hand. "You two look beat. Why don't I see if they're done with me for a little while? That way I can run you over to the resort ferry, and you can cross over to the city."

I looked up at him and nodded.

He walked away back out into the night.

"I like that man," Cat said, watching him.

"I do too."

"He might be a keeper."

"Oh? Like your Quincy?" I teased.

She leaned back in the chair and pulled the blanket around her a little tighter. "I haven't made that call yet."

"What?" I asked. "That Quincy isn't a keeper?"

She shrugged. Her smile was as wicked as I've ever seen. "You know I just keep him around because I'm too lazy to go out and look for another one. Don't you?"

"Sure you do."

"And he is sort of nice to look at sometimes."

"Err." The sound of a foghorn rumbled beside me, and I looked up, way up, to see Lurch, still in elf-cos. He held my coat out to me. In his hands, more like the big round heads of tennis rackets than anything else, the coat looked like a child's garment.

"Oh, Lurch, thank you."

He nodded and handed Cat's to her.

After a few more minutes, Jack pulled up next to the building in one of the resort's maintenance pickups. I got in beside him, and Cat rode shotgun.

Normally it took about half an hour to get from the resort to where the ferry boarded, but in the dark and mud and rain, we were on the road an extra ten minutes. It was still raining, so we sat in the truck with Jack while the ferry returned.

Jack walked between us with an umbrella. He took a good look around then leaned his face down and kissed me.

I heard Cat sigh before she turned and boarded.

The kiss lingered a short while, and when he pulled away, I missed him. Dating the boss hadn't turned out to be easy, especially with Jack's history. He'd come to Louisiana from New York because of an unintentional indiscretion with his boss's wife. Poor Jack. And what did he do when he got here? Why, he fell for someone he worked with, namely me. And even if The Mansion's owner, Harry, had sort of put his stamp of approval on our relationship, we both needed our jobs too badly to put them at risk even a little bit. But it wasn't easy being around him and not being able to touch him or kiss him or even stare into his eyes for too long.

"Good night," he said.

"You too," I said. "Sleep tight. Don't let the bedbugs—"

"Thanks," he interrupted, grimacing.

Jack stood on the dock and watched as the Mystic Isle ferry pulled back into the strong, swirling currents of the Big Muddy.

Cat and I walked to the front of the ferry to gaze at the lights of the Crescent City shimmering in the river water and casting reflections onto the clouds above the city. The air blowing back in our faces was cold and heavy with mist. Downriver a light bank of fog rolled in from the Gulf. The sounds of Christmas carols Dixieland-style were faint but growing louder the nearer we came.

I leaned against the railing and took hold of it with one hand before realizing it was wet. Melancholy overcame me, and my eyes began to burn. "Slim was a nice man," I said, my throat tight.

Cat took hold of my free hand and curled her fingers around mine. "He was. Why would anyone kill him?"

I could only shake my head. "Not just anyone. Knowing Quincy, after what Slim's wife said, I'd lay odds he's going to be asking Valentine a bunch of questions."

Cat sighed. "He's bad that way, y'know."

"There's no way Valentine would have run that poor man down. Heck, that woman cringes when she has to cut up a chicken. Tries to get the staff to do it whenever she can."

We landed and walked through the light rain to Decatur where we stood under the awning of the Café du Monde, watching a few adventurous tourists braving the December weather to get in some Christmas shopping—or holiday drinking.

A cab came by, picked us up, and took us home to our awesome apartment on Dumaine Street. Rain sparkled on the bricks under the courtyard lights as we let ourselves in. Our boy, Satchmo, our wonderful black kitty, ran up to greet us, rubbing himself against our legs and rumbling softly, like a tiny Harley.

We took off our coats and hung them on the rack by the front door.

Cat kicked off her shoes and headed straight for the kitchen. "Tea?"

I shivered and headed for my bedroom. "Don't you know it!"

While the water heated on the stove, we both changed into our warm jammies and slippers then headed back out to the kitchen just as the kettle began to sing. Cat put bags in to steep. I went to the cupboard for a couple of almond biscotti then we sat at our farm-style kitchen table, sipping and munching.

"It's still bothering me, that woman talking about Valentine that way."

Cat doctored her tea with cream and sugar. It wasn't the usual recipe for chamomile, and didn't even sound good to me. But Cat listened to her own melody more than most of us and was the kind of girl who could eat anything, anywhere, anytime and not gain an ounce. "It was kinda weird, wasn't it?"

"You gonna tell Quincy to leave Valentine alone?"

"I can tell him," Cat said. "Whether or not he's gonna listen is another matter altogether."

We didn't talk much after that—too depressed.

It wasn't long before we both began to droop. From the TV in the parlor, a familiar theme signaled the beginning of one of the late-night talk shows.

The resort was full of holiday guests, and almost everyone was busy. But my schedule during the holidays had always seemed to lighten up, and this year was no different. I had only one client scheduled for the next morning. He was a regular and had commissioned me to design a phoenix rising from the ashes for his back. The appointment was scheduled for ten a.m. Cat said she had a full morning of tarot readings, but neither of us was looking forward to going in to work Wednesday morning. After what had happened tonight, it wouldn't be pleasant.

CHAPTER FIVE

———

I staggered out into the kitchen the next morning bleary-eyed and grumpy after having lain awake most of the night obsessing over what happened to Slim. Every time I'd dozed off, a flashback would pop into my head, and I'd be wide awake. What should have been an evening of triumph and celebrating over a successful money-raising campaign had turned into something dark and sad and even scary. Even Satchmo had given up and gone in to sleep with Cat.

Cat and I showered and dressed and walked up to Decatur where we ordered a couple of big old mugs of chicory coffee and split an order of scrambled eggs and andouille sausage at a local coffee shop. The rain from the night before had washed everything clean, and the sun and crisp December air made sitting outside on the sidewalk at a café table the best option. The sidewalks were charmingly empty since most of the tourists who'd be out trolling later hadn't hit the pavement yet. When we'd eaten, we walked over to catch the dedicated Mystic Isle ferry, the same one that had brought us back to the city last night.

It was just docking up, so we stood and waited to board while it was secured. The day conductor, George, had a mad crush on Cat. She was sweet to him and good-natured about it, even though her heart belonged solely to the good-looking Cajun deputy with the cocky attitude.

"Mornin', ladies." George swept his Mystic Isle cap off his tousled hair, swinging it low in front of him, and followed it down into a gallant bow, extended right leg and all. "Your loveliness brightens our river crossing like the first light of dawn." His tendency to wax poetic was one of my favorite things about George.

"Why, thank you, George," we said together even though we both knew it was Cat he was speaking to.

Two women from resort housekeeping and the kitchen worker I'd met the night before, Aaron Bronson, boarded. Aaron was dressed in street clothes, loose-hanging faded jeans, a tight white T-shirt, sweatshirt-grey hoodie, and cool kicks that were probably knock-offs of black leather hi-tops from one designer or the other—knock-offs were all that made any sense on a kitchen helper's salary. His hair was all kinds of messed up, and it looked like he hadn't had time to shave. I'd never seen him cross on the ferry before and wondered why.

George lowered his voice. "I heard 'bout the trouble they had at the resort last night. A cryin' shame, dontcha know."

We both nodded.

Several more employees and a few others I didn't recognize boarded. One was a nice-looking guy who I figured to be in his early twenties. He looked like a slimmer, paler version of Jake Gyllenhaal with sandy-colored hair and grey eyes behind a pair of black-framed Buddy Holly glasses. He smiled at us when he boarded. It was one of those smiles you'd think about even after it was gone—slow, lop-sided, personal, like maybe it was the sight of you that made him smile. I was curious about him. I'd noticed him at the resort several times before. The man knew how to dress, and it was pretty obvious he had the pocket change to let him wear what he wanted. He wore a black leather jacket that looked soft as a baby's butt, as my Grandmama Ida would have said, over a slinky black button-front shirt and tight black jeans. Moto boots toughened things up so he didn't look like a dandy. He went to the far side of the boat, slid into a seat, hauled out his phone, and got busy on it.

As we pulled away and headed cross-river, Aaron walked up to me. Last night, in the monkey suit with his hair slicked back, he'd looked more mature. Now, with the sun on his face, there was a boyish air about him, and I could see he was maybe about thirty, when last night I would have said older.

"Hi, Miss Hamilton. We met last night. Aaron Bronson?"

"Sure," I said. "I remember." He wasn't the kind of man a girl would forget that easily.

"Pretty awful what happened last night."

I nodded, not exactly happy to be reminded.

"Did you know the man who died?"

Another nod. "He worked at The Mansion for the last couple of years."

"I didn't know him," he said. "I'm sorry for your loss." He took hold of my hand and patted it gently as his voice trailed off. "How are you doing?"

Oh mercy me, good-looking and thoughtful too? I needed to find a woman for him. He could be too good for someone to let slip through her fingers. And the "Barbie" doll he'd had with him last night didn't suit him. At least I didn't think so.

"I didn't sleep well," I admitted. "But thanks for asking."

His blue eyes held concern. "I knew you'd be bothered. Just in the short time we were together last night, I got the impression you're a sensitive woman," he said.

He was a little too familiar, and I thought maybe he might be hitting on me, but then he said, "I hope today goes well for you," and he turned and crossed back to the other side of the boat where he sat on a bench and looked out over the fast-moving muddy waters of the mighty Mississippi River.

The crossing only took about ten minutes. The shuttle bus was waiting when we disembarked, and we all rode in relative silence to the resort. I didn't know if the quiet was out of respect or worry or shock. Whatever. One of our own had been taken. It looked intentional, and with the missing bags of toys, gift cards, and cash, it looked like nothing more than cold-blooded murder motivated by greed.

The only person showing any liveliness at all was the well-dressed good-looking young guy who'd plugged in his earbuds and was carrying on an animated phone conversation as he looked out the window at the lush Louisiana bayou that was, we heard over and over again, being slowly overtaken by the encroaching Gulf of Mexico. While it wouldn't be for a long, long, long while, I surely knew when the bayous were gone, they'd take a way of life with them.

We pulled up under the portico where the sight of three squad cars and several law enforcement officials walking around set everyone on the bus to buzzing.

"Looks like more of the same thing we had last night." Aaron was up and out the shuttle. He stood by the door, holding out his hand to me first then Cat as we stepped down off the shuttle.

"It's a crying shame," I said. Cat nodded in agreement.

Cat, Aaron, the other employees, and I began to head around the building to the side entrance that led to the employees' locker rooms where we changed into our respective costumes. Cat and I broke off from the rest of the group when someone called out Cat's name, and we looked around to see Quincy heading toward us.

"Q," she said, moving in for a brief hug. "Are you making progress?"

He kissed her on the forehead and nodded. "We are," he said, "some anyway, and we're just 'bout to make ourselves some more. Gettin' ready to fingerprint all you wicked hotel people."

"Fingerprint?" I asked. "Us?"

"'Fraid so." He shrugged. "We're of the mind that one, it had to be an inside job, you see. Somebody knew Slim, Papa Noël, had that big ol' bag full of valuables. And this morning we got us a better look at the tracks of the vehicle that run him down. And the ME from 'cross the river, she confirmed it. Whoever did this nasty thing, they run him over. Then they turned around and they run him over again. And they take the bag, and not everybody who was here knew 'bout that bag. Just some people, mostly who work here. So, ladies, I been thinking I need to fingerprint all you people who work here who had previous knowledge of that bag."

I squinted at him. "I don't like the sound of that. You think it was someone who works here? Someone we know?"

"Oh, yeah," he said.

"But why do you need fingerprints? What are you trying to match?"

He shrugged. "Why, only the prints we lifted off the hotel utility van we found out by the old boathouse." He arched his brows. "You know, dat one with the front-end damage. Dat same one somebody needs to get holda the company keys to drive?"

I gasped. "Oh, Quincy, you've already found the truck that hit him?"

"Why, chère, don't you know I'm the best there is when it comes to homicide investigating?"

"I do know that," I said, "but I also know I want you to disregard what the Conner woman said about Valentine. She had no reason to say that, and you got no reason to pay any mind to it."

He just shrugged, but I could tell by the look in his eye I'd probably have been better off not having said anything.

Cat and I left Quincy to his work and walked back around to the side of the building. We went in and headed down the short hall, through the mud room where we hung our coats above several pairs of muddy rain boots before going on into the employees' locker room and staging area.

Like the folks who worked at those famous theme parks around the world, many of us wore costumes—Cat, the tarot card reader, looked like a gypsy when working, a fabulous, bling-layered gypsy; Fabrizio, when doing his séances, was decked out in a turban and mystical white Nehru jacket; my look was similar to Elvira, Mistress of the Dark, with a V-neck slinky black gown with a big stand-up collar that fanned all the way around the back of my neck. The waiters, waitresses, bartenders, and other service people dressed according to the theme of their environment. Lurch wore a three-piece black suit suitable for a butler, but it made him look more like a funeral director from Brobdingnag.

We didn't talk as we undressed, but as Cat pulled the gauzy boho-style blouse over her head and tied the fringed scarf around her waist, she said, "Does it bother you?"

"What?" I turned so she could zip my costume up the back. God forbid I ever had to try to get dressed for work by myself.

"That Quincy thinks it was someone…" She looked around. "…you know, someone here."

It was a sobering thought, one I didn't want to dwell on. "You bet it does."

"Good morning, girls. What a nice, sunny day. Cold, but still, after the way it was last night—and I'm not just talking about the rain, if you know what I mean—I'm really grooving on the clear skies and bright sunshine."

We both turned. "Morning, Stella." Stella by Starlight breezed into the room, her hands moving and her face as animated as if life was a drug and she was high on it.

"I'm so late this morning. I've got my foxy gambler this morning."

"Foxy gambler?" I sat down and gathered one nylon, pulled it on up to my thigh then did the same with the second before pushing my feet into the Mary Jane slippers I wore while working.

"Oh, sister, haven't I told you about my Mississippi River gambler?" Stella asked.

I stood and smoothed my costume skirt. "I don't believe you have, Stella."

She was out of her street clothes—that coincidentally looked a lot like Cat's gypsy costume—and was getting dressed in her silky maroon and gold Mumbai-style tunic and pants. "Zachary Jones." She sighed. "Oh, man, he's a total fox. Young for me, maybe even for you girls, but that cat's got it going on."

"And the punch line is…?" I prompted her, looking at my watch. I only had about fifteen minutes to get to Dungeons and Deities, my shop, and set up for my ten o'clock.

"No punch line. Zachary's just, well, far out. Too bad he's all business. The dude's too uptight, needs to loosen up, and if I was fifty years younger, I'd be just the woman to get him real nice and loose. And if he's open-minded, I still could be just the woman."

Cat laughed. "You're something else, Stella."

Stella lowered her voice conspiratorially and leaned toward us. "Zachary wouldn't dig it if he knew I was talking to you about him. He runs his own business, makes sports book. A ton of money in it. He da man. Comes to me at least four or five times a week to get his chart done, and the Saints', and the Pelicans'—sometimes I even chart the ponies running out at the track. Groovy, right?"

"Right," I said. "And how does it work out for him?"

"Stella by Starlight knows her stuff," she said, shrugging and smiling, like her prowess was not something to be questioned—and for all I knew, maybe it wasn't. "And I must be as good as I think I am, or at least Zachary thinks I'm as good as I think I am. Else why would he come around so much?"

"We all know you're the real deal, Stella," Cat said, spinning the dial on her lock.

Stella laughed. She had a great laugh, one of the best I'd ever heard, hearty and deep down in her throat. "Fifty years ago, I'd have said he was coming around because of my great legs, but these days, gotta be the down and dirty scoop he gets to make his odds and place his bets. Lately, my boy's had some trouble making collections. He's got some serious change hanging out there he can't collect."

All three of us finished together and headed out into the public areas of The Mansion, where the holidays were still in full swing, even if the atmosphere was more subdued than it had been before someone had run down one of ours.

"Your new shop everything you hoped for?" I asked Stella as we entered what I called the auxiliary section of the resort that had been added on to the main plantation residence.

"I love it," she said. "Right on."

She'd only recently moved across the hall from my Dragons and Deities tattoo parlor into a bigger space with blue-neon stars and Stella by Starlight over the door. It was gorgeous. Inside, starlit blue satin drapes sparkled under special lighting like moonglow. A small round table sat center-room where Stella cast astrology charts and counseled her customers.

We stopped outside the open door. The expensively dressed guy who'd crossed over on the ferry with us sat in one of the chairs. He turned around when we walked up and smiled. "Miss Stella," he said, taking off the glasses and looking at her with those soft grey eyes before ducking his head.

"Zachary," Stella's voice sounded kind of dreamy as she sashayed on in, suddenly once again the young woman with great legs she'd mentioned earlier in the conversation.

And I could see why he wound her clock up. Zachary stood, coming to his full height, like a cat waking and stretching from a nap in the sun. "I was wondering where you were, Miss Stella," he said, all sweet and Southern.

No wonder Stella had such a crush on him. College-age and fifty years her junior or not, as she'd said, he was a total fox.

I looked up and saw my own client, Chance Walker, stopped in the lobby, surrounded by half a dozen fawning women.

I turned and hurried into my own space and got ready for him, turning off the sanitizer I always left on overnight, booting the computer so I could show him the sketch, and pulling ink colors. I hoped he liked it.

This would be the second time I'd ink Chance Walker. He was a recently career-resurrected actor, having made a complete and utter comeback after years of drug abuse and rehab. This last one finally took, and he was on the comeback trail. His current series filming across the river in New Orleans was a smash hit. His reborn celebrity was what had given me the extra few minutes of fan chat I needed to get ready for him. It was also what had motivated him to ask me to design a tattoo that would celebrate the resurgence of his acting career—thus the golden phoenix rising from red and purple flames I'd be inking over his right upper arm and spreading its wings over the front and back of his shoulder.

He walked in, grinning, and I giggled like a kid, but not because I was star struck. Because I was psyched about my beautiful design.

"Hey, Chance," I said. "Say w'at?"

"Say w'at?" he said back to me. He'd told me he loved it when locals talked the talk with him, since he was still "studying the lingo."

I had him strip off his shirt and plopped him down in my chair, pretty much oblivious to his half-naked status.

Apparently, I was the only one because when I turned around to get my ink gun, there were over a half dozen women and girls standing in the open doorway, all breathing hard.

Behind them stood Jack Stockton, and he wasn't looking nearly as impressed with Chance's muscles as the others standing in my doorway.

CHAPTER SIX

———

Chance seemed to love his rising phoenix so far, but he'd turned out to be less of a tough guy than he'd originally figured. Sweat had beaded his brow at the sight of the needle, and when blood started to ooze in spots, he'd clenched his teeth and begged me to stop and let him take a break from what he called "the agony and ecstasy of it all."

We'd only been at it about forty minutes at that point, but I understood. Some people just had that reaction. He promised to come back in a half hour.

"Sure," I said, "but don't forget to stay away from the alcohol, aspirin, and ibuprofen until after we're done. That'll just make it worse in the long run."

I walked out onto the veranda, and the mournful tones of the funeral dirge set me to humming. Personally, I wished they'd have left the dang thing turned off, but now that the police and other first responders had quit wandering in and out, the guests probably expected it. Lurch was in the process of loading luggage into the trunk of a car for departing guests and posing with a family for a selfie, a child hanging off each arm like little monkeys. Lurch wasn't smiling, but I happened to know he probably loved it. The man had more selfies than all the Kardashians put together.

It was a beautiful day weatherwise, clear skies, clean air, temps around sixty. On the surface everything looked like a normal December day at The Mansion, festive decorations, excited families, and regulars who thought spending time with mediums, fortunetellers, and magicians was the perfect way to spend the holidays.

But most of the guests were unaware of the tragedy that had occurred the night before, and just under the surface crept an unsettling vibe among those of us who did know. Slim Conner had died in a cruel and violent way, and the evidence pointed at someone who worked here. Someone I knew? I shuddered.

Just inside, the double doors to the main salon opened, and Cat walked out, or rather stomped out, which was pretty hard to do in her costume slippers. I heard her footfalls all the way across the hardwood to the front doors as she came up to me on the veranda.

"Quincy wasn't just kidding when he said they figured it was one of us who killed Slim," she said, her cheeks flushed, nostrils flared, and her eyes bright. "Everybody's getting fingerprinted, including me."

"And me?" I asked.

"Oh, yeah." I could tell by the tone of her voice she was hurt and angry. "Wouldn't you think a man might be sensitive enough not to haul his girlfriend in and fingerprint her in front of God and everyone?"

"Well, he has to—"

"Oh, no you don't, Mel," she warned, a slim index finger and red-polished nail pointing in my direction. "Don't you go trying to soothe me. I'm enjoying this hissy fit way too much. Let it flow."

"I'm so sorry, darlin'." It was Quincy. "Sheriff Dickerson wouldn't let me get by with lettin' you slide. I gotta do my job f'sure."

He put his hand on the back of her neck and rubbed. When she looked into his big brown eyes, I could tell she wasn't angry any longer, but her folded arms stayed where they were, and her pouting lower lip stayed where it was too. "Oh," she said, sighing. "I know."

"You need me in there too?" I asked.

He didn't take his eyes off Cat's face but nodded. "Pretty soon."

It was then that a female deputy I'd met the last time there was a death at The Mansion came up the porch stairs and laid her hand on Quincy's arm. It was hard to miss the flare in Cat's eyes and the resultant smoke coming out of her ears.

"Q?" The deputy's voice was soft, sweet, and seductive as a siren's call. "We found something in the employees' area. You better come and have a look."

Quincy didn't seem to notice that she'd all but invited him to her place for the evening and maybe even breakfast the following morning with that sugary tone of voice, but I did, and I was pretty darn sure Cat did too.

Quincy, who hadn't yet taken his hand from the back of Cat's neck, gave one more small rub before asking Cat, "You taking a lunch break, sweet?"

Cat nodded.

"Want to join me after I see what Sergeant Mackelroy here needs from me?"

Cat's eyes narrowed as she looked at the diminutive, uniformed brunette with the big blue eyes. "By all means, Quincy…" She dragged out his name. "See what Sergeant Mackelroy *needs* from you." As the two officers headed back down the steps and veered toward the side of the main building, she turned back to me. "That one's been sniffing around him for I don't know how long. I may have to do something about it fairly soon now."

Jack's voice came from behind us. "Yeah, sure." I turned around. He was on his cell phone and had stopped dead just inside the door setting off multiple rounds of the funeral dirge. He just stood there, listening to what was being said on the other end of the conversation. After the fourth time of hearing Chopin's "Funeral March," I went inside a couple of steps, took hold of his hand, and pulled him out onto the veranda. A girl can only take so many times hearing that in a row.

He went on. "All right, please tell Mrs. Richards I'll be right there." He ended the call and sighed. I knew him well enough to be able to tell that something was bothering him.

"What's wrong? Want to talk about it?" I snuck a peek at my watch. There were still about ten minutes before I had to head back to Dragons and Deities and face Chance's hemophobia and fear of needles—there's a big word for that too, but I never could remember what it was.

Jack ran his hand through his dark hair, took a deep breath, and let it out. I loved the way his hair looked when he did that. It made him appear as if he'd been outside in the wind. But one of the things I loved most about Jack was his smile—big and wide, it creased his face like the sun splitting open the morning sky at dawn. There was no smile this morning.

"There's been another theft." His frustration was evident. "The Richards in the Magnolia Suite upstairs in the main building called the front desk about half an hour ago and reported Mr. Richards' camera bag was missing from their room when they came back from breakfast."

"Again?" I asked. "Oh, Jack, just what you need. Like you don't have enough to do."

"Mmm," he mumbled. "Yeah, well, it comes with the territory. She told the front desk that the cameras and lenses were worth several thousand dollars. Her husband's a professional photographer." He looked out past the front lawn where the police units were parked. "Shouldn't have to go too far to find a cop to report it to." He surprised me by dropping a light kiss on my lips before turning and going back inside. Jack never kissed me at The Mansion, at least not where we could be seen—he must have been really preoccupied to have done it. And it was understandable.

Over the last few weeks, there had been a series of thefts from guests' rooms, one almost each and every day. Camera bags, like the one just reported, but mostly expensive jewelry people were careless enough to leave in their rooms. Some other odd items had gone missing as well but on a smaller scale.

No leads had turned up, and both Jack and Harry Villars were stumped, as were the deputies investigating the thefts.

I could tell it had been bothering Jack a lot.

"I thought you had a full day with the actor," Cat said, pulling me back from my thoughts.

"Oh, geez!" I checked my watch again. Five minutes past the time I was supposed to be back at the tattoo parlor to meet Chance. "I'm late. Gotta go. Have a nice lunch with Quincy."

I turned and rushed back through the main lobby and took the hallway that led to the auxiliary wing where my little corner of the world was located. Sure enough Chance was standing outside the door. He looked up when I approached, and I could have sworn I saw him swallow hard and blanche.

Poor guy. Maybe this was something he should have thought about before he commissioned the tattoo. But he was too far into it to stop now. Half a bird wouldn't fly.

"Ha!" I made myself laugh, but Chance looked so pitiful I sobered up immediately, took him by the hand, and led him back into Dragons and Deities like an executioner leading a condemned man to the gallows.

At the rate Chance's tattoo was going, I'd still be on it after the new year had rolled over. He'd only lasted twenty minutes the second go-around and had asked me to hold off a couple of hours this time to let him "get my feet back under me."

I agreed. He'd turned so green while I was working on him I was afraid he was going to upchuck, and that was never a pleasant proposition.

At least I was now done with inking the golden part of the phoenix and only had a few more hours' work on the layers of other colors and the flames.

I had two hours to kill, so I thought about heading over to the Presto-Change-o Room for some lunch but then changed my mind. The fact that Slim wasn't there working would just have depressed me, so I stopped at the coffee bar, snagged a cappuccino and a croissant, and headed in the direction of the employees' lunch room.

I sat down at a table across from Aaron. A yummy-looking fried shrimp po'boy sandwich was on a wax paper wrapper in front of him with a side of Valentine's famous Cajun coleslaw and a glass of lemonade.

It made my lunch look pitiful.

He was reading something on his phone but looked up as I sat down. "Hi, Melanie," he said.

"Hi. It's just Mel."

He looked at my croissant and coffee. "I have half this sandwich I haven't even touched yet."

I smiled. "Oh, thanks, but I'm not all that hungry. Been thinkin' about Slim and what happened, you know."

"You sure?" He held up the half sandwich he was working on. "Pretty good stuff."

"I'm sure."

"So, Mel," he said. "You're a tattoo artist?"

"Mmm, that would be me."

"You like it?"

"I do. Art of any kind gets me going."

"Is that right?"

I told him about my degree in fine art and how I painted when I had time.

"You sell any?"

"Some."

And then I told him about the hours I spent at Jackson Square with other artists when I had a day off from The Mansion or from donating my time at St. Antoine's.

He leaned his chin on one hand and seemed to be giving me his full attention. It was sort of flattering that he was so interested.

But when Valentine Cantrell walked into the kitchen, all that changed. Heck, his eyes even lit up. He jumped up and pulled out a chair.

She gave him a special Valentine smile before she sat down with her The Mansion at Mystic Isle coffee mug. It was one of those benevolent smiles that made a person feel like they'd been blessed by the Pope or something.

"Thank you, Aaron. You're always such a gentleman." She winked. "And good-looking too. We need to find you a good woman. One that can cook and make you happy."

He blushed. "Aw, who'd want me?"

Okay—so like I'd said before—he was good-looking, thoughtful, and now humble too? Valentine was right—we needed to get this guy hooked up with one of our friends. He seemed too good to let languish away dating someone like the Barbie doll he'd been with at the company dinner last night.

We sat and talked awhile, and I complimented her on last night's menu. She talked about how determined she was to somehow come up with the $65,000.00 she needed for Benjy's first full year at the music academy.

Aaron stayed quiet, seeming to hang on Valentine's every word.

After only a few minutes, Quincy and Sergeant Mackelroy came in, Quincy carrying a pair of yellow rain boots in a plastic bag.

All three of us turned to face the two cops.

"Valentine?" Quincy began, nodding first at me, then Aaron. He walked up to Valentine and held up the bag. "You recognize these?"

She leaned down and peered at the plastic bag before nodding slowly. "Those are my rain boots," she said. "Why are they so muddy, young deputy?"

"That's funny," Quincy said. "I was just 'bout to ask you that same thing, Valentine. If these are your boots, these same boots with your name written inside in permanent marker, then why is the mud caked on them mixed with blood?"

Her mouth dropped open, and she looked up at him, gasping. "Caked with…?" Her voice trailed off.

"And, why," Quincy went on, "did we find the keys to a resort utility van inside them? The same utility van that was used to run down Slim Conner last night?"

Valentine began to shake her head. "I don't—"

"And why, Valentine, were your fingerprints found inside the same utility van?"

She found her voice. "I drove that van yesterday morning to help Odeo Fournet get some of my big catering pans out of storage and bring them over to the kitchen."

Quincy's face was troubled. He was a fan of Valentine's, as star struck by her as any of us, and this was probably bothering him a great deal. "Valentine, please tell me you have an explanation for the blood on the boots and the keys to the van being tucked inside them. Please tell me your desperation didn't send you out into the night to run down Papa Noël and take his bag with all dat money just so's your boy can go to that fancy music school across the river."

"Have you lost your ever-lovin' mind, Quincy Boudreaux? Of course I didn't kill Slim. He was my friend."

"We heard he was your *friend*," Sergeant Mackelroy spoke up, her tone self-satisfied and a little bitchy. "Slim's wife, Diane, she said you and Slim had been spending a lot of time together, and—"

"How would she know that?" Valentine said. And I could only reach across and lay my hand on hers, shaking my head in a signal she shouldn't address anything they had to say. Things weren't looking good for my friend. Not good at all.

Mackelroy went on. "Mrs. Conner said her husband told her he'd been visiting you at your home in the evenings but that he wasn't going to be making that trek anymore. Was that something else you were having trouble with, Chef Cantrell? Were you angry he'd told you the affair was over?"

"Affair?" Valentine's voice shook. "What affair? Slim had come to me for advice. And that. Is. All."

"Advice?" Quincy said, his voice hopeful. "What kind of advice would that be?"

Valentine shook her head. "I can't say. It was confidential, and Slim wouldn't want me to talk about it."

Quincy snorted. "Confidential? Woman, the man, he dead."

Valentine shot a withering look. "But I'm not. Not yet anyway."

Two more sheriff's deputies walked into the lunchroom and stopped six or so feet behind Quincy and the female deputy.

My heart began to beat fast and hard. I didn't like the way this was shaping up at all. What the heck was the matter with them? They couldn't seriously believe that Valentine, the essence of Mother Nature with a dose of Creole spice thrown in, had it in her to harm someone with anything more deadly than her sharp tongue, much less slam over someone with a van then go back for a second run at him.

"Quincy?"

He looked over at me.

I went on. "You're just covering your bases, right? You can't really believe Valentine had anything at all to do with poor Slim's death."

He didn't answer at first, but regret clouded his eyes, and then he said, "It don't matter what I believe. The evidence is what matters. We have Valentine's muddy boots with what maybe will turn out to be the victim's blood on them, the keys to the vehicle that ran over him hidden inside dem boots, her fingerprints and nobody else's inside the van that was used as the murder weapon—that's evidence. The victim's wife? She said Slim, he was seeing Valentine on the sly but that he was done with all dat and called it off, and Valentine herself, she said she needed some big money to get her boy into that music program—and that's motive." He turned once again to Valentine. "Sorry, but I need to know where you were last evenin' between five o'clock and seven o'clock?"

She put her hands to her face. "I was here until Benjy finished. Then I took him home. Well…" She raised her gaze to his. "…not home. I took him to my sister's place for the night. And then I was heading back here for the dinner."

Aaron and I looked at each other, and it was like we could read each other's mind. Valentine had never shown up at the Christmas party. Her chair had remained empty all night.

Valentine went on, her voice, normally husky and whiskey smooth, was squeaky. "But I never made it back here. I went through a dip in the road where the rainwaters had risen, and my car flooded out. By the time I got it started up again, I'd missed dinner, so I just went home."

Quincy looked like he might be sick. I sure felt that way, and from the look of astonishment and dismay on Aaron's face, I figured he was feeling that way too.

Quincy's voice was low. "Chère." He cleared his throat. "Valentine, please tell me there's someone who can vouch for you."

The shake of her head was barely perceptible.

"So you don't have an alibi?"

She chewed her lip.

"I'm so, so sorry." Quincy stepped back. "Valentine Cantrell, you're under arrest for the murder of Phil Conner aka Slim Conner."

The two deputies who'd come in a few minutes earlier got Valentine on her feet and began to cuff her, while Sergeant Mackelroy, who I was beginning to hate, recited the Miranda rights.

Valentine's calm and centered presence shattered with the sound of the handcuffs locking. A small squeak of fear sounded at the end of each breath, and there was nothing less than pure panic in her eyes as she looked at me. "Oh, Lord. Mel, call my sister, and make sure she's still got Benjy. Tell her what's happened."

Aaron was on his feet and trying to get between Valentine and one of the deputies. "Chef. Chef, what should I do?"

Quincy took hold of his arm. "Stay back here now. This won't do you no good, and it won't help Valentine."

Aaron jerked his arm away. My eyes went to his clenched fists.

"Shh, Aaron." It was Valentine. "It'll all be good. I don't have anything to worry about. I didn't do anything wrong." She gave Quincy a hard look. "Did you hear that, Chief Deputy Boudreaux? I said, 'I didn't do anything wrong.'"

Aaron took a step closer to the two deputies surrounding her, and Valentine turned to me. I finally got my wits about me and took action, standing and moving around to Aaron, laying my hand on his back where the muscles were tense. Still breathing hard, he stood back.

"You want to help me?" Valentine said to Aaron.

He nodded, looking miserable, and I could suddenly see how strong his feelings were for her.

She went on. "Then you help Melanie figure this out. She's done it before, and she'll get to the bottom of this before you know it." One last look back at me then, "Mel, you get on this. You hear? I need you, girl."

CHAPTER SEVEN

————

Yes, I had done it before—with the help of my boyfriend slash boss, Jack Stockton, and my girlfriend slash roommate, Catalina Gabor. We'd had to muster up to save another friend from the clutches of the evil sheriff.

Looked like it was up to me, Melanie Hamilton, Wonder Woman—nope, that wouldn't work—I didn't have the figure for the outfit. How about Melanie Hamilton, Supergirl—better? At least there was a cape to wrap around me on those days when I gave in to my cravings for too many beignets.

They'd taken Valentine out right away, and it broke my heart to see her. She was scared. It had been in her golden eyes, but she'd held her head up and her shoulders back and tried to pretend it was no big deal.

I'd have been wailing and crying my eyes out.

Aaron had watched her go, his mouth set in a hard line then he'd turned to me. "So?"

I looked around—behind me then to each side. No one else in the room, which meant he must have been talking to me.

I arched my eyebrows and pointed my finger at my own chest.

He nodded. "Yes, you. Chef said to work with you to prove her innocence, and I'm no detective." Something in his eyes made me feel sorry for him. He said it again, "So…?"

"Uh…" *Glib, Mel. So glib.* "Well…I…" *Get your act together now, Mel.* Valentine, in her own words, needed me. And, yes, I'd come in handy helping to catch a killer once before, but I'd stumbled into that one. And here I was sort of being shanghaied into service. No way I could say no to Valentine Cantrell. She could just look into my eyes, and I'd go into a trance, lift my arms, and zombie-walk, saying, "Yes, Master. Whatever you need, Master. Right away, Master."

Funny thing was, even though I felt forced into it, I really wanted to help her. I didn't any more think Valentine had run down poor Slim than I had, and truth be known I was more a likely suspect than the gentle, nurturing soul she was.

I looked up at Aaron who was still just standing there seeming to be waiting for some direction from me. Sad thing was, I didn't have any direction, didn't have a clue where to start.

"Okay," I said. "First things first. She wanted me to call her sister." I picked up my half-eaten croissant, left the cold cappuccino on the table, and started for the door.

"Where you headed?" Aaron called after me.

"To the human resources office," I said over my shoulder. "I have to get hold of Valentine's sister and let her know what's going on so Benjy's being cared for."

"Well, what should I do?" He sounded a little lost.

"Can you go to Jack Stockton's office and tell him what's happened? Number one, someone has to be put in charge of the kitchen until this all gets straightened out. And two? Well, if I know Jack, he's gonna want to help out."

I was halfway out the door when I heard him say, more to himself than to me, "Jack Stockton? What the heck can that big city stiff do to help?"

I should have stopped and turned around to stand up for my man, but the urgency in Valentine's eyes and the desperation in her voice when she'd begged me to call her sister kept my feet moving forward. All I had time for was a staccato statement thrown back over my shoulder. "You're gonna be surprised all Jack Stockton brings to the table."

I went straight to HR and got the number for Valentine's sister, who she'd listed as her emergency contact, and headed outside to the veranda to make the call. Lurch was just coming on for his shift and was busy loading up one of the resort's luggage carts that Harry Villars had custom-made and shipped in from someplace in eastern Europe—the running joke was Transylvania, but maybe not. The carts looked fairly normal for the most part, open and carpeted on the bottom, big wheels for smooth handling. It was the tops that were a little unusual. Skulls (not real ones, at least I didn't think they were real) sat above the arched tops instead of decorative finials, and mini skeletons dangled from nooses beneath them. Lurch always looked right at home pushing them.

The phone call to Val's sister was quick and to the point. She'd shrieked and uttered a few words that one generally doesn't hear in polite society then promised to cover Benjy for as long as it took to get this all straightened out.

"Your sister's my friend," I told her, "and I'm going to do anything and everything I can to get her out of this mess. If you need anything, call me." I gave her my cell phone number.

When I walked back into the lobby, Aaron was wandering around, looking lost. I caught up to him. "What did Jack say?"

He lifted his arms. "Nothing yet. He wasn't in his office." He glanced up at the enormous gothic brass clock that hung behind the reception desk. "But I gotta get back to the kitchen. Without Chef Cantrell, they're going to need every spare hand they can get if dinner service is going to be done on time."

"Okay," I said. "You do what you need to do. I'll look for Jack."

He walked away, and I picked up a house phone and called Jack's office.

"Jack Stockton's office. How may I help you?" His assistant, a fifty-something woman who guarded Jack's door like a lion at the gate, always sounded a little defensive when she answered as if the person on the other end of the line had darn well better be the President of the United States or at the very least the owner of the resort.

"It's Mel," I said.

Her voice softened. "Hello, honey." The third dignitary on her short list was little old me.

"Is Jack in his office?"

"No, he isn't, dear. I believe you can find him in the Presto-Change-o Room. He said he was feeling kind of low and thought maybe a cheeseburger and some Dixieland might lift his spirits. But I bet a visit from a certain young lady might perk him up even more."

Jack's and my relationship wasn't a secret, but we didn't like to acknowledge it to the rest of the staff. Dating the boss was tricky. "Okay," I said, "Thanks. I'll go see if he's still there."

I crossed the lobby, rounded behind the big curving staircase that led to the upper floor and the fancy suites that had been carved out of the second floor rooms, and walked into the Presto-Change-o Room.

It was the first time I'd crossed the threshold since last night, and it struck like a physical blow that I wouldn't ever see Slim behind the bar again. I'd miss his smile, his jokes. I'd miss seeing his happy face, his white beard always so immaculately trimmed. His beer belly had always seemed to make him look a little like a pregnant woman in the wizards' robes all the Presto-Change-o bartenders wore. But he'd taken it in stride and had even joked about it with customers who'd thought it was hysterical to ask when he was due.

Slim had been popular with both the staff and the customers. He'd had a great singing voice, gravelly and jovial. His version of "Hello, Dolly!" was requested at least two or three times a night.

Desi Lopez de Monterra was playing that song now, working the keyboard of Zelda, the ancient piano Harry had discovered in a second-hand store over in the Quarter. Ever since the incident with the so-called "haunted" piano, Desi had been the resort's go-to guy when a solo piano player was needed to fill in here and there. He'd been coming in for day shifts during the holidays. If Desi fit in anywhere it was The Mansion at Mystic Isle during the holidays.

He was a small, slim Latino guy who favored oxfords with Cuban heels and loud clothing. His work attire for the day was a two-piece Christmas green suit with red and white candy canes all over it, red patent lace-up shoes with those fancy high heels, and a red fedora with a candy cane stuck in the white hatband. While it hurt my eyes to look at him, I couldn't look away.

He lifted one hand from the keys, waved, and blew a kiss when he saw me walk in then went back to his rollicking Dixieland version of "Winter Wonderland."

Jack sat at one of the window tables that looked out over the pool area, which had been decorated in a haunted Christmas motif with skeleton Santas and elves, spiny tinseled trees with twinkling zombie lights, and big plastic floating gators with glowing red noses. In the winter, they kept the pool at eighty-eight degrees, and the steam rising from the water looked appropriately like swamp gas.

Jack had pushed away a half-eaten cheeseburger. I went over and sat down across from him, snagging a Cajun french fry off the plate.

"Hey there." He looked at me and smiled, and my heart expanded with emotion.

I'd never had feelings for a man like those that I held in my heart for Jack Stockton. He was handsome, sure. Any girl would be attracted to him because of that, but what got me the most about him was his kindness and consideration of the staff who worked for him. When he'd first come to the bayou from the Big Apple, there had been a pool started as to how long the Yankee would last—no one took a bet it'd be longer than a couple of months. But my Jack had proven them all wrong. He was here. He was doing a great job. And he was well-liked by the staff.

I looked around before reaching across the table, taking a brief hold on his hand, and squeezing. He squeezed back.

Over his shoulder a couple of tables over, I could see Stella by Starlight and her bookie, Zachary Jones, in a conversation over coffee.

I didn't know how else to break it to Jack, so I just said it straight out. "Valentine's been arrested."

He sucked in a deep breath.

"They found blood on her muddy rain boots, the keys to the utility van that ran over Slim stuffed in them, and she can't come up with an alibi."

He just stared at me, then, "Tell me you're kidding."

"If I were, would you think it was funny?"

Shaking his head, he looked around the room like he was grounding himself—as if he were hoping he was in the middle of a bad dream. "How could anyone believe she'd be capable of something like that? But especially Quincy? He adores her."

"I know," I said. "It hurt him to do it. You could see it, Jack. But with all that stacked against her, what else could he do?"

He didn't have an answer, so he just shrugged.

"Anyway, somebody needs to be put in charge over the kitchen until she gets back."

He sighed and nodded. "I'll take care of that. Her sous chef, Louise, has been working under Valentine long enough it shouldn't be a problem."

"Sure," I said. "And besides, Valentine won't be tied up long." We both winced at my terminology. "I mean, she'll be back to work real quick."

"That's right," he said. "We have to believe that, don't we?"

"So, are you going to help me?"

"Help you what?"

"Help me prove her innocent, of course."

He just stared at me.

"Well, since you helped me last time there was a killer to catch, I figured you'd be up for it again."

He gave a little laugh. "Sure. Why not. I always say there's nothing like a good murder investigation to get the blood stirred up."

"Mel?" It was Stella.

I looked over at her table. She and the bookie were both looking at us intently.

"Did I just hear you say that Chef Cantrell was arrested for killing Slim?" she asked.

I thought we'd been keeping our voices down. She must have hearing like a cat.

"Slim Conner?" The bookie sounded surprised. "Did you just say they arrested someone for murdering Slim Conner?"

Stella gave him a look I wouldn't have been able to label as anything but a warning. What the heck was that about?

The bookie cleared his throat and added, "I mean, I know Slim Conner. Bartender, right? Someone killed him?"

Stella lifted her arms, palms up. "We couldn't help but overhear. What a bummer."

Jack stood and went over to their table, looking down at the bookie. "Mr..."

"Jones," Stella's client said. "Zachary Jones."

"Mr. Jones, there's been a terrible tragedy here at The Mansion, and I'm sure you understand the sensitive nature of such an occurrence. I'm going to ask you to keep what you've heard today to yourself."

Zachary pushed his glasses back up onto the bridge of his nose and began to nod his head really fast. "Sure. No problem. I just...I just would like to know everything I can about this. Like I said, I know him."

"He was a friend of yours?" Jack asked.

The bookie looked at Stella then back up at Jack. "Yeah. Right. He was a friend of mine, all right."

Jack studied the man in front of him, but no more than *I* studied him. Zachary Jones was keen on what was going on, zoned into it, and locked on.

"Who's this person they arrested?" he asked.

"It's a matter of conjecture, Mr. Jones. The police have taken someone in for questioning, that's all. I wouldn't want to start any rumors about a person who's probably going to be asked a few questions then released. I'm sure you wouldn't either. So once again, I'm going to ask you to not mention what you've overheard here today." He paused. "I bet there's something the resort can do for you in consideration of your discretion."

Zachary looked first at Stella, then at me, and finally at Jack. "I bet there is. I'll keep in touch."

CHAPTER EIGHT

———

Whatever Stella's client Zachary Jones had in mind as compensation for keeping his cards close to his chest about what he'd heard, it never came to light. Bookies were notorious players, and if there was an angle in it, it was logical he'd play that card soon when it suited him.

He and Stella had left together and weren't gone more than five minutes before Jack and I set to talking about our plans for Christmas Day when we both planned to take in midnight mass at St. Antoine's, hook up with my mama, a few others, and Grandmama Ida at her place for a réveillon dinner. After that, we'd all go over to St. Antoine's Children's Home to help with the Christmas morning festivities—snacking on shortbread and hot cocoa while the children unwrapped whatever presents could be scraped together, since Papa Noël's big red sack had been stolen.

"What are we going to do about replacing the cash we collected for Nicole's bone marrow transplant?" Jack shook his head, his voice grim, his jaw set angrily.

"I don't know," I said. And I didn't. We'd all worked so hard during the drive to get together the toys and gift cards for the orphans. It was a big loss but not as big a loss as the life of a friend or the subsequent loss of the cash earmarked specifically for Nicole's procedure.

I looked up as Sergeant Mackelroy appeared in the doorway to The Presto-Change-o Room and stood looking around. She came forward when she spotted us.

Small with what was a shapely figure camouflaged beneath a bulky Kevlar vest under her uniform, she was still feminine and cute.

She tilted her head and smiled at Jack, fluttering her lashes. It looked like maybe Cat wasn't the only woman who'd have to keep an eye on her man when the sergeant was around.

The eyelash thing went on so long I honestly thought about asking if she had something in her eye, but that would have been catty, and no one wants to look that way in front of her boyfriend. But still…*meow, y'all.*

"Mr. Stockton?" When did she acquire that Scarlett O'Hara simper? "Chief Deputy Boudreaux is still busy with the suspect and said I should ask you to join me in the boathouse. Maybe you can verify our discovery there."

Jack pulled his hand away from mine and stood, and I narrowed my eyes at the deputy before saying, "I'll just come along too, if that's fine with you."

"Show us the way, Sergeant," Jack said.

She didn't say anything but shot me a look then took hold of Jack's hand and backed away in a *come with me to the Kasbah* move if I ever saw one. "Call me Pammie."

I felt like a third passenger on a bicycle built for two as I followed along behind them. Jack seemed unaware of my discomfort. That didn't mean anything. Most guys were oblivious to things like that, and besides, he was so preoccupied with the murder and the room thefts and the loss of the donations from the charity drive he didn't have time for my silly insecurities. But that didn't keep me from taking a couple of quick steps to catch up to him and take hold of his free hand.

Pammie took the hint and let go of his other hand, straightening her shoulders as her gait took on a more purposeful stride.

As we went through the lobby, I couldn't help but notice the eerie background music usually heard throughout the public areas had been replaced with Christmas music, specifically, "Grandma Got Run Over by a Reindeer."

Jack looked at me, his expression ironic. "Remind me to have that taken off our playlist, at least this year."

I nodded. "Good idea."

We crossed under the portico, out onto the lawn area, and then beyond to the old boathouse that had been converted into sort of an all-purpose utility building. Resort mechanics worked on paddle boats, airboats, and other equipment there. It was also a general storage facility for landscaping tools and materials. Odeo Fournet was sort of king over that part of the realm as all his grounds keeper gizmos were kept there.

One of Jefferson Parish Sheriff's Office SUVs was parked on the service road, and a male deputy stood by the door waiting for us.

We went inside. The lower level of the old boathouse consisted of two water bays where boats could be pulled in under the roof and lifted out of the water for maintenance. That section butted up against a portion that was built over land and basically housed a tool shed complete with workbenches, winches, and lifts extending out into the open area where boat motors could be repaired. That took up about half of the interior lower-level space, the rest of it being dedicated to bags of fertilizers, gardening tools, mowers, and seed bags. Dark and musty with shafts of sunlight slanting in at odd angles, it smelled earthy and moist, like a root cellar. The slap of the water against sides of the walls and walkways was the only sound.

Creepy, much? It was right in keeping with the rest of the resort.

Sergeant Mackelroy—oops, my bad, *Pammie*—led us to the far side and up the stairs to the second level, which was even darker and spookier than the downstairs.

It was less humid—drier—up there, and extra chaise lounges, cushions, tables, sun umbrellas, and other poolside furnishings were stored there during the off-season when fewer were needed. One portion housed crates full of enormous baking pans and serving dishes. Other areas were used for storing Mardi Gras, Halloween, and other specific decor. The holiday items would be brought back here after they were taken down.

"There." Sergeant Mackelroy pointed to an area in the middle of the room occupied by about thirty or so cardboard boxes. "You see?"

The printing on the outside identified the contents of the boxes as Jack Daniel's, Captain Morgan, Absolut, Johnnie Walker, and other brand names—it was all liquor, or as Harry Villars would have said, "Ardent spirits, potable courage, fortified libations, alcoholic beverages."

Jack walked over for a closer look, and I followed.

He stood over the boxes, scratching his jaw as he looked at them. "What the heck are these doing way out here?"

It seemed rhetorical, but Pammie answered. "We were wondering the same thing. Didn't seem like you'd want something this valuable and easily disposed of in an unsecured location like this."

"Well," Jack said. "This place is locked most of the time, but there are several people who have access to the keys. The main one being Odeo Fournet, but there's no reason for these cases of liquor to be out here."

"So you're saying this doesn't belong out here."

"Yes. That's exactly what I'm saying, and if you don't' mind, I'd like to get someone out here to explain it to all of us."

Odeo was summoned to the boathouse from where he'd been working on adding gravel to one of the access roads that had gone horribly muddy during the previous night's rain.

He came up the stairs slowly, followed by the deputy who we'd seen outside when we first arrived.

He stood with his hat in his hand, twisting it around.

"Mr. Stockton, sir. You need somethin'?" Odeo's skin was like ebony, his teeth way whiter than piano ivories, his scalp as hairless and round and smooth as polished onyx. He was big, over six foot four if I'd had my guess, and strong—physically beautiful. His process might have been a little slower than most. He always seemed to think carefully before he spoke, and when his words did come, they were measured and slow. Odeo was easily overstimulated and cried like a child whose candy had been taken away over the most minor issues. His gaze landed on the liquor boxes, and his eyes went wide. "Oh, man, what's they still doin' here? I done told him to leave off that stuff."

"What, Odeo? Who?" Jack asked.

"Slim. Poor dead Slim. I done told him I didn't want him selling this stuff out o' my boathouse no more. And he was supposed to get all this out of here."

Sergeant Mackelroy, back in sheriff mode, stepped in. "Slim Conner, the murder victim? You're saying he was trafficking stolen liquor from this boathouse? And you're saying you knew about it and didn't report it?"

Odeo's expression was filled with fear and confusion. "It wasn't no stolen liquor. He was just selling what was rightful his. His commissions, he say, for doing good at selling drinks in the Presto-Change-o. But I told him to clear it all out, else I might get in trouble for letting him run it out of this place. I knew and he knew that it wasn't right."

"Slim told you these boxes of liquor were his commission?" Jack said.

Odeo nodded, looking from Jack to me to the deputies.

I kept my voice low. Odeo looked so scared I didn't want to alarm him any further. "Could Slim have been stealing from the resort?"

Jack shrugged. "I'm assuming so. There was no commission, certainly not cases and cases of liquor. He had plenty of access to the key to the storeroom. He probably had a healthy list of buyers since I'm betting there's a big market down here for underpriced tax-free booze."

"And you'd win that bet." Pammie added in her two cents.

Jack turned to Odeo. "If you knew he was doing it, Odeo, why didn't you come to me with it? Knowledge of this makes you complicit."

"Compl-what?" Odeo stammered.

"It means you participated in what he was doing, Odeo," I said as gently as I could. "It means you sort of took part in it too."

"Oh, no, ma'am, Miss Melanie. I didn't take no part in it. Once I found out about what he was doing, I said, 'Slim, you need to clear all this out, and don't be doing it again.' I told him, 'Or else.' We shouted about it too. He said he needed a lot of money, and he couldn't help doing this bad thing, and he wasn't going to stop it. He pushed me, and I had to hit him to get him off me." Shame and guilt filled his eyes before he hung his head. "I just couldn't have Slim selling out of my boathouse. And I told Slim he'd better be careful, or I was going to do something about it, and he sure wasn't going to like it."

Pammie Mackelroy opened her mouth to speak, but Jack cut her off. "You threatened him, Odeo? You hit Slim Conner and threatened him?"

Odeo took a minute and finally said, "I reckon I did do that, and I meant it too. But I had to. If he wasn't going to leave off doing this bad thing in my boathouse, well, I could have got fired. And I like this job."

CHAPTER NINE

———

I left Jack, Odeo, and Sergeant Mackelroy—since the contraband liquor gave her something to think about besides Jack—and the other deputy to hash out the issue of the purloined alcohol and headed back to Dungeons and Deities to finish Chance Walker's rising phoenix. It took the rest of the afternoon. When I finished, he made a good effort at springing up, but the process of getting to his feet was accomplished more in jerky increments than in the swift, panther-like swagger the general public associated with Chance. The ink, if I said so myself, was incredible—all gold and red and purple, and once the swelling, bruising, and scabbing healed up, it was going to be something to see. I wondered if they'd cover it up in his shirtless scenes on the series.

He gave me a really nice tip, $300.00, for my efforts then kinda hunched over and cringing, he shuffled out. "I think I'll check at the front desk and see if I can get a room for the night. I don't want anyone to see me on the streets in case I pass out. Not good for my image."

I didn't smile. He hadn't done well with the pain. It didn't mean he wasn't as macho as some of my other customers, at least not to me. But I could see it bothered Chance a lot. I decided not to say anything about it to anyone.

I closed up shop and headed out to the lobby to wait for Cat whose last appointment was running late.

About twenty-five or thirty members of the Circle of Ravens, a pagan group that showed up every year to celebrate the season, were milling around in the lobby. Jack said they had chartered a bus to take them over to St. James Parish for a night of ritual around a bonfire on the levee, for which Jack and Harry had received special dispensation from the parish to hold on the winter solstice instead of Christmas Eve when the other bonfires would burn in the normal Christmas Eve tradition.

Jack said they'd seemed to be everywhere around The Mansion since the weekend, gearing up for their big night of the year. They were pretty darn easy to pick out in a crowd. The men all had long hair and beards, and if it weren't for all the heavy jewelry, robes, and other accoutrements, they would have looked like people from the *Duck Dynasty* family. The women all wore hooded robes with bell sleeves and had long, untrimmed hair with sprigs of holly and what might have been actual tree branches stuck in it.

Jack walked up to me and slung an arm around my shoulders. He watched the Ravens mill around, a confounded look on his face. "Gotta say I never had a group like this stay at the hotel in Manhattan."

I laid my hand on top of his and laced our fingers together. "You mean the Circle of Ravens never booked their Yule festivities at that slick business property you used to manage?"

He grinned and shook his head.

"Well, my lands, son," I said. "Why not? You wouldn't build them a bonfire on the banks of the Hudson?"

"You having fun picking on me, woman?"

I looked up at him. He ran his free hand through his short, thick hair, making some of it stand up straight. My lips wanted to feel his against mine. My body wanted to feel his warm arms around it. But we'd agreed—none of that romantic stuff would go on in front of guests. It wasn't easy.

When Jack had first arrived at The Mansion, he'd been a little stiff—unsure, he'd said, of whether or not he'd be able to assimilate. And he hadn't, not really. He was still a big city Yankee boy trying to make a go of it in the Louisiana bayou among the bizarre cast of The Mansion and the eccentric guests who arrived on a daily basis to feed their paranormal fixations. But when we'd all seen how even-handed and good-natured Jack was, we'd rallied around him, accepted him, and taken him in as one of our own. Especially me. I just wanted to be with him all the time, but we both worked long hours, especially Jack, and finding alone time to learn about each other didn't come as often as either of us wanted.

"Mr. Stockton?"

I let go of Jack's hand, feeling a little guilty about how cozy we probably looked to an outsider.

It was Diane Conner who had walked up to us and addressed Jack. She looked haggard, her hair stringy and dull, her face tired and older than when I'd seen her the night before. And why wouldn't she? Her husband had been murdered.

Jack's voice was kind. "Mrs. Conner, how are you doing?"

She shrugged. Her grey eyes were flat, lifeless, but her tone was just as sharp and a little witchy like it had been last night. "Oh, just dandy. How do you think I am?"

Jack cleared his throat. "I know this must be the hardest thing you've ever had to go through."

She frowned, looking up at the ceiling as if she were trying to recall, and I half expected her to come up with another time in her life that had been harder. But instead, she scratched her chin and said, "Who on God's green earth are all these weirdos running around here?"

Jack's eyes widened. He may have thought the same thing himself, but hearing it out loud when the weirdos themselves were within earshot was another matter altogether. "It's a...a special interest group, Mrs. Conner."

"Hmmph." She snorted. "Freaks if you ask me. And that one in particular."

I looked in the direction she pointed. It was Lurch, skin made up greener than the Grinch, wearing a suit of holly leaves, a hat of holly leaves, and yes, shoes of holly leaves. His legs were snug in the same green tights he'd worn at last night's gala when he'd been dressed as Papa Noël's elf. He lumbered through the lobby, thumping the rubber end of a staff decorated with, what else, holly leaves.

The Ravens cheered when Lurch showed up, circled around him, and led him to the front entrance. He wasn't smiling.

I looked at Jack, who lifted his hands. "Slim had agreed to be the Holly King for the group. I had to find someone else last minute, and Lurch already had the tights."

It was at that moment that Diane let out a shriek and lunged at Jack, wrapping herself around him. "Oh, Lord have mercy! It's him. Save me, Mr. Stockton. Don't let him get me!"

Jack and I both looked up. The lobby was pretty much empty since the Ravens and their so-called Holly King had left on their chartered bus that would take them out to the levee bonfires.

The only person I saw Diane could possibly be talking about was Stella by Starlight's enigmatic client, Zachary Jones, the bookie.

Diane swung around behind Jack then leaned out, peeking around him as the bookie made his way toward the front entrance then out.

Hyperventilating and wheezing like an old bellows, she gasped, "What in the Sam Hill is he doing here?"

We both stared at her. "Mr. Jones?" I asked. "Are you talking about Zachary Jones?"

Her eyes were dilated, and it was obvious her fear was all too real. "I don't know his name, just that he's a demon seed, a mad dog, and Slim was scared to death of him. And now..." Her voice caught. "...it looks like he's come for me too."

That cute but nerdy college boy didn't look like a mad dog to me. "But...why would he come for you? And why was Slim afraid of him?" I was confused.

"That man's been at my house. *My* house," she shrieked. "And Slim and him fought, almost went to fist city. Young guy like that would have beat the living snot out of my husband. I don't know what that stupid husband of mine did to get that guy so ticked off at him that he'd come around like that and poke his finger at Slim, and yell, and carry on like some bull on a rampage. Slim wouldn't tell me. But it must have been bad. Slim, he never had the sense God gave a goose, anyway. Not a brain in that man's head. But whatever it was he wanted from Slim, it looks like he's coming after me now."

"Mrs. Conner—" I began.

But she cut me off, grabbing hold of Jack's lapel and shrieking. "Oh, dear God, what am I gonna do? I'm in danger, Mr. Stockton. Don't let him kill me."

Jack walked her over to a bench and had her sit.

As upset as she seemed, any other woman would probably have been sobbing her eyes out, but there wasn't a tear in sight. Her mouth twisted. "No good Slim Conner. I was crazy to think he'd ever be any darn good. Working all the time, and for what? There never was any money. And this wasn't the first disreputable-looking character who ever came around our place giving Slim a hard time. But this one, he was real mad. Madder than any of the others, and he scared Slim, and he scared me too." Her hands shook, and she clasped them together.

"I'm sorry to see you like this, Mrs. Conner," Jack said. "Can I get someone to drive you home? Maybe you'll feel safer there."

She looked up at Jack. Her eyes, so dull before, were now filled with terror. "Are you freaking nuts? Why would I go home knowing that crazed son of a gun is out there stalking me like a wolf?"

I couldn't do much more than just stare at her. Zachary Jones didn't exactly seem like a wolf to me, more like one of the Geek Squad guys who drove around in Volkswagen Beetles.

Her reaction to him had been real, but that wasn't what I'd found so intriguing.

I couldn't help but remember how interested the bookie had been when he'd heard Jack and me speak of Slim's murder and how he'd said they were just "friends." Going to someone's house, getting into a shouting match with them, poking them in the chest, and nearly coming to blows didn't sound all that friendly—but maybe that was just me.

Jack got up from beside Diane and went over to the front desk. I followed him.

"Lucy," he said.

The reception clerk on duty walked up. "Yes, Mr. Stockton?"

"If we have the room, I'd like to offer Mrs. Conner another complimentary night."

Lucy checked the computer. "No problem, Mr. Stockton. We have room. I had to double-check because Chance Walker, you know, the actor?" She blushed. "He just booked a room for a couple of nights. Left word not to disturb him unless he called down for a doctor."

I snorted.

Jack gave me a look.

"I'll tell you later," I said. "I think having Slim's wife stay here is a great idea. There's something going on there we need to figure out. It's pretty plain the way she talks about him that she didn't really like Slim much, and there's gotta be more to the story about Stella's client and Slim coming close to a knock-down, drag-out." I paused. "Don't you think?"

He looked thoughtful for a minute, obviously considering what I'd said. "Okay," he said. "I'll ask Harry first, and if he says it's all right for her to stay here—"

"He will. I know he will. He wants Valentine back here as bad as we do, if not worse."

"You're probably right. And Mrs. Conner seems to want to be here anyway." He narrowed his eyes. "Are you thinking she might be a suspect? Wasn't she at the dinner last night?"

"Yes, she was." Sure I was talking out of school, but Valentine's freedom was at stake, and all bets were off. "But she didn't come to the table until well after six, and she was all kinds of sweaty and messed up, like she'd been doing something physical, you know, like maybe running down her husband with a van."

CHAPTER TEN

———

Jack offered to walk Diane back to her room and see her safely inside.

I stood by with my hands crossed in front of my waist, calm and smiling like a nicely mannered Southern girl until they were out of sight, and then I went tearing back to the auxiliary wing like a bat out of hell (which I probably looked like in my long black costume with the stand-up Count Dracula collar). I had to double-time it if I was going to catch Stella before she left for the night.

My timing was just about perfect. She was locking the door as I ran up. She turned in surprise.

"Hey there, girl, what do you have your panties in such a bunch about?"

I stopped and took a minute to catch my breath, thinking it might be time to partake in a little regular exercise. "I wanted to ask you a couple of questions about your client Zachary Jones."

"Oh." She looked skeptical. "Like what?"

I explained what had just happened in the lobby, how Diane Conner had nearly fainted when she spotted Zachary walking through the lobby.

"She freaked out?" she asked.

I nodded. "Big time."

Stella looked at me for a minute as if she might have been considering whether or not talking about her customer was somehow a breach of trust. "I don't know if I should..." she began.

"Oh, come on, Stella. What can it hurt? It's not like you're his lawyer."

"Funny you should say that. Zachary has actually threatened me with his lawyer if word ever gets back to him I was talking about his business. And, after all, he is my client."

"Yes," I said evenly, "but Slim was your friend."

After another long pause, she shrugged and hooked her arm through mine. "Well, come on then. Walk me to my car, and we can talk on the way. I guess it doesn't matter since I've already mentioned it to you before, and I know you're the soul of discretion anyway."

"Sure." I crossed my fingers and asked her what she knew about Zachary Jones and whether or not there'd been a connection between him and Slim Conner.

"Remember. You can't tell anyone you heard this from me. That little geeky bookie is one of the resort's most lucrative customers. Not only does he come to see me nearly every day to cast his chart, sometimes if it's late when we finish up, he'll stay over if there's a room for him. I don't want to lose his business, and neither will Harry or your Cap'n Jack."

My mouth hung open. "How'd you know I call him...?"

She just gave me a mysterious smile.

We walked a few minutes in silence before she began to speak. "I don't know much, but what I do know is that Slim Conner liked to bet on the horses. A lot. And he wasn't good at it. He owed money to Zachary. And he was behind in his payments."

I stopped walking and stared at her. When she realized I'd stopped, she did too. "Stella, if it was enough money for him to go out to Slim and Diane's house and threaten him if Slim didn't pay up, it might have been enough money for Jones to make an example out of Slim so his other customers wouldn't default on their payments as well."

"I don't want to think that about a gorgeous hunk of flesh like Zachary, but who knows what lurks in the hearts of men?" She shrugged dramatically. "But, like I said, I don't know much."

"But that doesn't work out," I said. "Zachary Jones wasn't here last night." I added, "Was he?"

"Not as far as I know, at least not inside at the party where we were," Stella said.

We'd come to the stone wall on the kitchen side of The Mansion that set off the employee parking lot. Stella used her gate key to go in.

Stella lived in a two-bedroom frame house on Fisher Street over in Lafitte, only a hop, skip, and a jump from The Mansion. The house was painted haint blue to keep the evil spirits away, and the living area was lifted up out of flood danger on stilts. She drove her 1965 VW minibus back and forth. Every time I saw it, I marveled she could still get parts for the thing. Considering the minivan and my mama were the same age, the old girl was holding up pretty well—the VW, not my mama, although she was pretty cute too.

The outside of Stella's bus was painted in bright psychedelic colors of green, blue, yellow, and fuchsia with the sun and moon and shooting stars. It sat out under one of the Victorian-style pole lamps in the employee parking lot, looking like it belonged in a Pixar movie and might smile and come to life any second.

"So, whether or not he was highly motivated, if he wasn't here, it wasn't him who killed Papa Noël."

She took my hand and patted it. "Whatever you think, Mel. We all know you're the sleuth around here, but I didn't say it wasn't Zachary who killed Papa Noël, and I didn't say he wasn't here that night. I just said not as far as I know."

She turned before she got into her VW and asked, "You want to come over to the house and get high?"

"Oh, gee," I said. "No thanks, I'm good."

She shrugged, got in, and started the engine. I turned and went back around to the front of The Mansion. A bus was parked out front that looked a lot like the one that had taken the members of The Circle of Ravens out to celebrate the bonfires on the levee, but what was it doing back so soon?

Inside, a uniformed bus driver was talking to Jack and waving his arms around like something exciting was going on.

"You've got to be kidding," Jack said, running his long fingers through his short thick hair. "Just what I frigging needed."

"What is it?"

"The bus driver says the Ravens and the Cajuns are getting ready to rumble."

"What?"

"That's what I said." He looked at me, and I could see the exasperation. "What's next?"

It seemed like a rhetorical question, but I answered anyway. "Beats me."

He turned around just as Aaron Bronson wheeled a room-service cart out of the elevator.

"You," Jack said.

Aaron looked up.

"It's Aaron, right?" Jack went on. "You look like you can handle yourself." He wheeled around toward the front desk. "Lucy, get somebody out here to take that cart back to the kitchen, please."

Lucy picked up the phone.

"I'm gonna need somebody to help me," Jack said. "We have a bunch of guests about to get themselves in some hot water out on the levee, and I need to go out there and get it stopped before they find themselves in real trouble."

Aaron grinned and said, "Heck yeah, I'm game. In the army I worked on the bomb squad. These days I can use a little action."

I was struck by how handsome and strong the two men were, fierce and intense, and ready to go out and save the day. Why it was enough to make an old-fashioned girl swoon. But there clearly wasn't time for that.

"Mel," Jack said. "Run and get a first aid kit, and anyone else you can find who can help, then grab your clothes from your locker, and meet us back here. You can change on the bus."

"But who should I—?" But he was already on his way out the door.

I ran to the employee locker room, yanked open my locker, grabbed my jeans, T-shirt, jacket, and boots. Then I went to the main cabinet where a few towels, name tags, paper plates, plastic forks, and other things employees found a use for were kept, among them a well-stocked first aid kit.

As I headed back to the lobby, I ran into Fabrizio. He was still in costume, a white jumpsuit and cape, white patent leather boots, and a silvery turban with a big old fake diamond in the middle.

"Fabrizio, come with me. Jack needs us." I grabbed his hand on the fly and pulled him along behind me.

He came without a question. It was just the kind of man he was, always ready to help in whatever way possible.

As we headed across the lobby, I spotted Marvin Pendleton, the little elf who'd performed with Lurch at last night's gala. He was at the reception counter, and it looked like he might have been hitting on Lucy—in his elf costume. Oh, my, Catalina would be heartbroken at his perfidy.

"Marvin," I called out. "Marvin, come with us."

He looked up, startled. "Who, me?"

"Yes, you. Jack Stockton, the manager, he needs help. Please come."

Marvin came at a run and passed both me and Fabrizio.

Out front, the chartered bus was already running, Jack and Aaron already aboard.

Odeo was boarding just ahead of me. He turned and took my hand to steady me. "Mr. Stockton, he say they's having trouble out on the levee."

"I know," I said. "I hope we can stop it."

I clambered up the steps, Fabrizio and Marvin right behind me.

Jack was in the seat right behind the driver, and Aaron directly across the aisle.

I handed the first aid kit to Jack. "I'll head on to the back and get out of this costume."

As Fabrizio and Marvin headed up the aisle after me, I heard Jack say. "Okay. Not what I expected, but you guys will be great. Fabrizio, at least take off the turban."

And then, after a pause when all I heard was the engine running, the whoosh of the bus door closing, and the bells on Marvin's hat and elf shoes jingling as he made his way up the aisle behind me, Jack said, "Seriously? God help us."

I went all the way up the aisle to the last row, tossed my clothes and boots on the seat, and reached for the zipper on my dress.

"I could help you with that."

I turned around. Marvin was standing on the seat directly behind me, his hands in the air, making a zipping motion.

"Oh, no you don't." I said, pointing my finger back toward the front of the bus. "Go. I can take care of this myself. Thank you very much."

He sighed—"Just trying to help."—jumped down off the seat, and moped all the way back to the front of the bus, leaving me to shimmy out of my dress in the dark.

CHAPTER ELEVEN

———

After changing into my street clothes, I rolled up my costume, made my way up the aisle, and took the seat next to Jack, stopping to stash my costume in the overhead bin above him.

It took a little over forty minutes to make our way from The Mansion at Mystic Isle to St. James Parish along the banks of the Mississippi River, where Louisiana tradition held that December bonfires lit the way for Papa Noël making his way to all the good little boys and girls.

It was obvious trouble was brewing when we crossed over the levee and took in the scene.

The Mansion had sponsored the winter solstice event for the Circle of Ravens. It was meant to be a private party. The bonfire had been erected in the shape of The Mansion herself, complete with log pillars along one side to simulate the veranda pillars at the resort.

But the body count let us know that way more than the number of Ravens who'd left the resort were milling around on the levee.

The bonfire blazed, sending sparks into the dark, clear night sky. The tempers were also blazing. The robed Ravens and whoever else was out there were pushing each other around.

When the driver levered open the door, sounds of shouting and swearing assaulted our ears. Jack grabbed onto the rail in front of the seat and hauled himself up. My best bet was to leap up out of the seat and get out of his way.

It was a mini stampede as all five men left the bus and ran out onto the levee. I didn't know what else to do with myself, so I grabbed the first aid kit and followed.

The cold night air hit my face. The familiar smells of the Mississippi washed over me. Some people think the river stinks, but to me it smells like home and always will.

The bus driver jogged past me and leapt into the fray behind Jack, Aaron, Fabrizio, Odeo, and Marvin, who had all surged into the crowd and begun to try to separate the rabble-rousers.

There was a lot of shouting.

"Go back to your Sherwood Forest, ya freaks."

"Get the heck off me, Gandalf."

"Go back to the bayou where you belong, Neanderthal."

I got the impression it wasn't all as bad as it looked and sounded. The Cajuns were sloppy drunk and barely upright, and the Ravens weren't all that athletic to start with. Their idea of a brawl was using their staffs to knock the feet out from under their opponents then sitting on them.

It only took about ten minutes for the men who'd traveled from the resort to begin bringing people back to the bus. All the people who came with them were Ravens.

The Cajuns had begun to disburse on their own when police sirens became audible in the distance.

Everything settled down. Out on the levee, two of the resort employees, who'd probably been sent out early to the bonfire, stood watch over it as the mini Mansion imploded on itself, and the flames began to die down.

The solstice celebration was apparently over.

I reboarded the bus and made my way to the back to take an inventory of injuries.

All in all, the damages were minor. A few bloodied noses, some scrapes, folks who'd have trouble hauling themselves from bed in the morning due to bumped knees and elbows. Nothing major. No one wanted to make a stop at the local urgent care, and the conversation was pretty animated as we pulled back over the levee and headed back to the resort.

The bus was fairly full, so I took the empty seat next to Odeo.

We rode in silence for a few minutes until he said, "I surely hope Chief Deputy Boudreaux will be finding somebody to take to jail on account of old Slim. I truly like Chef Valentine.

She a fine lady. She didn't no more kill Slim than she be running for President."

Aaron had evidently been eavesdropping. "She is that. A fine lady. Have you decided to help her, Mel?"

I didn't hesitate. "Yes. I'm going to do everything I can to find out who really killed Slim. It couldn't have been Valentine. I just don't believe it. What motive could she possibly have had?"

Odeo made a little noise that sounded somewhat like a low growl. I turned to look at him in the darkness of the bus. The moonlight coming through the window cast a pale sheen over his dark skin. He raised one hand to rub over the top of his head. "Chef Valentine, she ain't got no motives. Heck, I got me more motives to kill that man than her."

I didn't like the way he said that. There'd been a quality in his voice that sounded almost like a confession. "But you didn't kill him. Did you, Odeo?" My voice sounded sharp even to me.

He didn't answer at first, and when he did it wasn't an answer, more like a dodge. "Well, I did hit him," he said. "I did do that. He wasn't a very nice man. They was lots of folks didn't like Slim. And I was one of them."

I sat back against the bus seat and tried to figure out if an enraged Odeo would have been capable of scheming to run over the man who was trouble to him. I didn't want to think it. His childlike manner had always made me fond of him. *Please don't let him be the one. I couldn't bear it any more than I could if it turned out to actually be Valentine.* And I had to wonder why it seemed my friends tended to get themselves in this kind of pickle.

Fabrizio was in the seat across the aisle beside Aaron, next to the window. He'd leaned his face against the cold glass. "Are you all right, Fabrizio?" I asked.

He turned away from the window. "I believe I am, my dear." He sounded pretty chipper for a man who wasn't used to having to stop such a fracas as the one at the levee. "I also believe I'll be sporting what you call a shiner in the morning."

"Oh, no," I said. "I'm so sorry."

"Not at all. It's my first, a battle scar I'll wear proudly until it fades away. Although I must say I am a bit miffed over the stains on my costume."

That made me smile.

Lurch was folded up on himself in the row behind Fabrizio and Aaron. He was doing quite a bit of his low, forlorn moaning. I understood. He wasn't the outdoor type to begin with, and the idea of the poor man being paraded around the bonfire in that leafy Jolly Green Giant outfit for everyone to see made me feel a little sorry for him.

He began to hum, low in his throat, and I soon recognized it as "99 Bottles of Beer." It wasn't long before others heard it and began to sing the words.

We'd gone through several rounds and were taking down and passing around even more bottles of beer by the time the driver pulled the chartered bus back under the portico at The Mansion.

* * *

When we'd arrived back at the resort and everyone had piled out of the bus and gone inside, under the lobby lights I saw that Jack had some bumps and scrapes on his face, as well as a little mouse swelling under one eye.

"Oh, no." I reached one hand to lightly tap it.

He flinched and pulled back. "Ow."

That settled it. My Cap'n Jack never complained. Never. I reached up, placed my hands on his shoulders, and turned him around. "We're going to your place and putting an ice bag on that," I said.

He didn't object.

Jack had lived in the honeymoon cottage on the resort property since he'd first been hired and moved to Louisiana from New York. I'd always thought it was meant to be a temporary arrangement between Jack and Harry Villars, but when he wasn't asked to relocate after several months, I got the idea that Harry liked having his general manager at The Mansion twenty-four/seven. It certainly helped when a crisis arose. Jack didn't seem to mind either. He was a hands-on manager who loved his job, and the honeymoon cottage, small and self-contained, was just right for a bachelor who worked long hours.

It was a three-room suite with a kitchenette—remodeled into a modern lodging from the original plantation kitchen. Jack had put his own stamp on things. There was a photographic poster of the Manhattan skyline Jack said he himself had taken from the top of the Empire State Building and had blown up. Posters of Phantom of the Opera and West Side Story hung over his bed. *And don't ask me how I know that.*

He sat quietly, eyes closed, on one of the stools at the kitchen counter while I ever so gently pressed a Ziploc baggie full of crushed ice up against his face. He laid his hand on top of mine and sighed.

After a few minutes, he opened his eyes, and I found myself staring into his dark gaze that spoke of his intelligence, good-humor, and kindness—and at the moment his desire for me.

"What a night," he said.

I laughed a little. "Have to say I've never been to a bonfire quite like that one before. Guess that's what you get if you deviate from the Christmas Eve tradition. If it's usual, you just sit around, eat gumbo and drink spirits, watch the fires and the fireworks, and get the little ones all excited 'bout Papa Noël coming."

Jack snorted. "Curse of the Circle of Ravens, I guess. Don't tell Harry I said this, but I kind of hope they don't come back next year."

"No luck. They come every year. It's one of the few places they're actually welcome, if they don't cross paths with the Cajuns that is. Yes, sir," I said. "God knows you don't fool with tradition when there's even one Cajun around. Those people are great believers in the past, tied to it even. And they're not shy about public displays of out-and-out disagreement."

"So I noticed," Jack said, rubbing his jaw wryly. "Who knew the Ravens could be so pugnacious when provoked."

"Pugnacious." I laughed. "Now there's a word you don't hear every day, city boy."

He laughed, put his hand around my neck, drew me closer, and kissed me. Jack was a good kisser—firm-lipped, just the right amount of pressure, no tongue unless he meant things to go further, which he apparently didn't tonight. And that was all right with me. It had been a long day, and I had a lot on my mind.

"This Zachary Jones guy," I began. "I've got my eye on him."

Jack took the ice pack from me and held it himself. "Should I be worried?"

"You know what I mean," I said. "I've got my eye on him for what happened to Slim."

With his free hand, he squeezed my shoulder. "Just teasing," he said. "If we can help clear Valentine, I'm with you on this. What do you have in mind?"

"That's just it," I said. "I don't know this guy. How am I going to get close enough to him to find anything out?"

"He's a bookie, right?"

I nodded.

"And from what you told me Stella said, his business is important to him, important enough that he spends a small fortune here having his astrology charts done to add his own good luck to the spreadsheets he uses."

Again, I nodded. "That's what she said."

Jack shrugged. "Seems pretty simple to me."

"I don't suppose you'd be willing to share your thoughts then."

He took hold of my hand, pulled me up, and began to hum Justin Timberlake's "Like I Love You." We danced a couple of minutes before I said, "Ok, so spill it."

He pulled me closer and put his lips next to my ear. "If you want to get close to a sports bookie, girl. You've got to place a bet with him."

CHAPTER TWELVE

———

After Jack walked me back to the resort, and the shuttle took me to the ferry, I crossed over and walked the few blocks to our place on Dumaine Street. The air was crisp and cold, the sky clear, but I couldn't see the stars until I rounded the corner off the busy, well-lit thoroughfare of Decatur onto Dumaine, and the only lights were the amber glow coming from residence windows.

We rented a two-bedroom from Mrs. Peabody who owned the three-apartment complex where she, our neighbor Beauregard Taylor, and Cat and I shared the lovely brick courtyard surrounded by the building. I let myself into the locked gate. Light from Mrs. Peabody's place and our place spilled out into the courtyard. Beau's place was dark. He tended bar at Thibadeaux's on Bourbon Street in the Quarter and was probably getting extra hours during the holiday season.

Cat was snuggled on the sofa in her robe and slippers, watching *How the Grinch Stole Christmas* on TV. Satchmo was curled up on her lap but jumped down and ran to greet me when I walked in.

Cat turned. "How'd it go?"

I took off my jacket and hung it on the coatrack just inside the double French doors that led me into the living room. "It was pretty exciting." I sat down at one end of the sectional sofa and toed off first one boot then the other, rubbing one stockinged foot against the other. "I've seen Cajuns brawl before, but who knew those long-robed tree huggers would be up to holding their own." I patted the empty spot beside me, and Satchmo jumped up and curled up, his head on my thigh. I scratched his ears. "Jack got a few scrapes and bumps."

Cat grinned. "Did you kiss all the boo-boos and make them better?"

I sighed. "Not all of them."

On the TV set, the music swelled and the Grinch's heart grew. We both stopped talking to watch. We both loved this holiday favorite from childhood.

When the credits began to roll, Cat switched off the TV. "Did you have something to eat?"

"Not yet," I told her. "You?"

"Scrambled eggs and andouille sausage. Still some in the skillet." She got up. "Come on. We'll heat it up."

I carried my plate out to the Mission-style table we'd stripped down and refinished when we'd first moved in. Cat sat opposite me with a cup of her favorite Waterfall chamomile tea that she ordered off the internet by the case. I'd filled a glass with almond milk. Neither Cat nor I would have ever been called good cooks exactly, but we both did a mean breakfast. And tonight was no different. "This rocks, Cat," I said, chewing.

She fluffed her hair. "Why, thank you, ma'am."

"What's on your calendar for tomorrow?" I asked. "I'm off, and I was thinking I might go 'round to one of those disreputable betting parlors. You know, see if I can't catch me a killer?"

"You what?" She practically choked on her tea.

"You wanna go?" I asked.

"Heck, yeah," she said. "I'm going straight to bed and setting my alarm. I wouldn't miss this for the world."

* * *

I got up the next morning and called Stella. She said she was still getting ready for work and sounded rushed.

"I have a plan," I told her.

"Good to know," she said, sounding impatient.

"I'm going to place a bet with your client Zachary Jones and grill him about where he was and what he was doing the night of Slim's murder."

"Oh, Mel, not really," she said.

"Yes, really. I don't buy that Valentine had anything to do with this mess, and not only do I want to clear her, I feel like when the killer stole Papa's bag, it was almost as if he was stealing from me. Those kids need the loot from that benefit, especially Nicole. A match could come up for her any day, and if money isn't there to help with the bone marrow transplant, it could mess things up real bad. And I know you want to help, Stella."

She was quiet for a while, and I began to think she might not answer but then, "What can I do?"

"You can tell me where your customer Zachary Jones runs his illegal sports book."

She swallowed so hard I heard it all the way from across the river in Lafitte, over the phone connection. "What makes you think I know where he runs his business from?"

I didn't answer, didn't figure I needed to. I gave her time to come to the inevitable conclusion.

Finally, "It's over on Bourbon Street, above a bar..."

She gave me all the details, and I wrote down every word she said.

After I showered and dressed in what I hoped was appropriate wear for sleuthing, a pair of black jeans, black boots, a long-sleeved black T-shirt, and a leather motocross jacket, I dug out my old pixie-cut black wig and put it on. It made me look like a thirteen-year-old boy, but at least maybe Zachary wouldn't recognize me. For good measure, I put on a pair of sunglasses to disguise my eyes.

I walked out of my bedroom to find Cat sitting on the sofa, waiting and wearing, honest to God, the exact same outfit, only with a blue long-sleeved T-shirt and long blonde glamour wig. It told me I'd chosen the correct wardrobe for the chore.

She stood and yanked down her jacket. "You ready?"

"You kiddin' me, chère?" I replied. "I was born ready."

We locked up and left.

*   *   *

Rue Bourbon, Bourbon Street. Obi-Wan Kenobi would have accurately described it as a wretched hive of scum and villainy. While I wouldn't have gone quite that far, Bourbon Street was definitely one of a kind. Cat and I pointedly avoided it most of the time, but of course when Jack and I started hanging out, I had to take him there. He'd heard all kinds of things about it. Most were true. He'd commented that even Times Square wasn't nearly so hedonistic. It was said to be Mardi Gras year round, and that there were places on Bourbon Street that never closed until the last partier had left the building, so people could drink and carouse around the clock if they wanted to.

Women with any common sense at all avoided going there alone at night, and even in the daylight, it could be a little iffy. I was definitely glad Cat had wanted to come with me.

The morning air was still brisk as it swept along the nearly empty sidewalks, quiet by Bourbon Street standards. Street sweepers had already made their rounds, so things weren't in a terrible state. The address Stella had given me for Zachary Jones's sports book was above a bar called Floozy's, just on the hetero side of the Lavender Line.

A confused and disheveled-looking guy sat on the curb in front of the bar, his head in his hands as a cop stood above him with one foot propped on the curb while he checked the guy's ID. The cop looked up as we walked by, his disapproval evident. Cat and I both smiled and went quickly into the bar before someone stopped to ask what a couple of nice girls like us were doing in a place like this.

The farther we went inside, the darker it grew. Tables and chairs were on one side, an old-style wooden bar on the other. A stale smell of beer and bar food permeated every nook and cranny.

An older guy sat at the counter nursing beers. Two middle-aged couples hovered over an order of wings and a few huge rainbow-colored drinks.

A woman behind the bar, leaning forward on her elbows, straightened as we walked up to her.

"Stairs?" Cat asked.

The bartender didn't reply until I said, "Looking for Zachary," then she pointed us to the back of the place where we found a flight of barely lit stairs.

I put my hand on the sticky bannister then pulled it off and looked at my palm before placing one foot on the first step. "So, here we go." I was suddenly nervous.

Cat was behind me, looking up, her eyes big and round. She gulped. "You first."

CHAPTER THIRTEEN

———

Up we went. After ringing a buzzer, we waited in an area on the second floor that had been recently upgraded. New brick pavers tiled the landing. The door itself looked fairly new and clean and was opened by a guy who looked like a contemporary of Zachary Jones. About the same age and demeanor, except this guy must have tipped the scales at over 250, and every ounce looked like solid muscle.

He didn't speak but stood waiting until I said, "I was told to ask for Zachary." Then he opened the door wide, and we walked in.

Cat grabbed the back of my arm, and I had to shake her off. "Geez, Cat."

We were led toward the back of the place where a bank of video screens lined the wall. On each screen was one kind or another sports event going on—football, basketball, ice hockey, car races, and one with a green screen with white letters that looked like an odds sheet.

Zachary Jones sat facing the screens, chewing on the end of a pen.

All around us, people were clicking away at computers and holding animated phone conversations. It was busy as an anthill.

The young guy who'd led us in spoke. "Mr. Jones, someone to see you."

Zachary swiveled around. He looked surprised to see us, but there was no flair of recognition in his eyes. "Hello," he said. "How can I help you?"

"We'd like to place a bet on a horse race," I tried to sound like I knew what I was talking about.

He grinned. "Oh, great. Well, Dan here can help you with that."

Dan, the guy who'd answered the door, gestured and said, "Right this way—"

I interrupted him, standing my ground. "I was told to ask for Zachary." I was pretty sure my voice shook.

Zachary leaned his elbows onto his knees and laced his fingers together, looking up at us. "And you are?"

"Um, Priscilla McGillicuddy."

"Do I know you?" he asked. "You seem familiar to me?"

"No," I said, hoping it didn't sound phony. "I never saw you before in my life."

"Who told you to ask for me specifically, Priscilla?"

"Slim," I said. "Slim Conner."

"Slim?" Zachary asked. "How do you—did you know him?"

I pretended not to know what happened to Slim and just shrugged. "Just seen him around here and there. You know."

"Huh." He stood. "I'm glad to help you." Then he led us to a computer station and sat down behind it. "Tell me."

"Well, we..." How was this sort of thing done?

Thank God for Cat, who'd found her voice and her confidence. "There's a filly running in the fourth today at the track. Gypsy Lady. She has good odds, and we'd like to place a cash bet on her."

He nodded, sizing up the two of us and held out his hand.

I fished around in my jeans pocket and pulled out a crumpled twenty-dollar bill, which I laid on the small table, smoothing it out with my fingers. "There ya go."

He stared at it. Then he looked up at us.

"That's your bet?"

"Well—" I looked at Cat. "Yeah."

After a beat, he began to laugh, and my face went hot. "What?"

Cat cleared her throat. "It's not enough?"

He stopped laughing after a bit and said, "Well, if you want my honest opinion, you and your twenty dollars would have a lot more fun making the trip out to the actual track. They take bets like this there."

"Hmmph." Cat narrowed her eyes at him. I could tell he'd gotten off on the wrong foot with her. She yanked her purse around and unzipped it, reaching inside and bringing out another twenty-dollar bill, this one in better shape that the one I'd given him. "What about now?" she said. "Will you take our money now?"

He studied her a minute and laughed a little before reaching for the forty bucks. "Sure," he said. "Why not? Who knows? You girls might roll this into something major and wind up being my best customers one of these days."

He explained the process to us. Our bet was on Gypsy Lady, a three-year-old filly, to place in the fourth race. If she came in second, the odds were such that our $40.00 would miraculously become $640.00.

"Really," I said, totally amazed.

"But if she runs anything but second," Zachary went on, picking up the two twenties, kissing each one, and then waving at us. "Buh-bye."

He laughed again. "I want to thank you girls for coming in. You made my day. It's been a while since I took a bet like this one, and it'd be a real kick in the pants if you win. So good luck."

I suddenly remembered why we'd come. It wasn't to gamble—Mama would have died if she knew—it was to get answers.

"We'll be sure to thank Slim for sending us, and if you see him first, tell him we said, 'Yat.'"

"Not likely I'm gonna see him anytime soon. You didn't hear?"

I batted my eyes until Cat poked me in the side. "Hear?"

"Slim's dead. Got knocked over a couple of nights ago out in the bayou."

Both Cat and I took in an exaggerated breath. "What? Slim Conner?" I gasped.

"You sure 'bout that?" Cat whined.

"Pretty sure," Zachary said. "They're saying it was murder."

"Oh, my," I said. "When was that?"

"Tuesday night," he answered. "Out where he worked. The Mansion at Mystic Isle. It's across the river over in Jefferson Parish."

"Wow," Cat said.

"How'd you hear about it?" I asked. "Were you there?"

He nodded. "I sure was. There was some big shindig going on, and I'd forgot all about it till I got there and saw my lady who I see over there wasn't working, so I turned around and came back here. But I was there for a little while. Slim, he wasn't working at his usual place then either. And, believe me, I wanted to talk to that man."

"You needed to talk to Mr. Conner about something?" Cat asked.

Zachary nodded absently while he clicked a few keys on the keyboard in front of him. "Oh, yeah, I needed to talk to him about 52,000 somethings," he said absently.

The noise I made in the back of my throat caused him to look up at me. "Money? Was it money? Did Slim owe you $52,000.00?"

His face was serious. "Your friend Slim was a real deadbeat, and I was a fool for letting it mount up like that. He even stiffed me on the interest payments." He smirked. "Now I know you ladies would never do something like that. Would you?"

We both shook our heads.

He went on, "Because if you did, well, I couldn't be responsible for any bad karma you might be creating for yourselves."

I didn't know what to say. Cat took hold of my hand.

"Well," I said. "I guess we better be getting on back home."

We both turned and hadn't taken more than two steps toward the door when Zachary's voice, harsh and imperative, cut right through us. "Stop!"

We both looked up at the only apparent exit, where Dan stood blocking the door, massive forearms crossed over his chest.

"Holy crud," Cat whispered. "We're gonna die."

But apparently not just then. Zachary stood and came around the computer station. "You forgot your receipt, Priscilla."

"Oh." Whew. "Thanks." I took it, and Cat and I double-timed it to where Dan was now holding open the door to let us out.

It was after ten thirty when we walked back out onto the sidewalk in front of Floozy's. Cat had an appointment at work, so she headed down to the ferry, while with my bet in mind, I splurged on a cab that carried me from Bourbon Street over to the Lower Ninth Ward and St. Antoine's Children's Home. On the way, I snatched off the sunglasses, took the black wig off my head, scrubbed my scalp with my fingers, and then fluffed up my hair.

Then I called Cap'n Jack. He was already hard at work in his office. "Hey, girl."

I sighed. Those words on another man's lips would make him sound like a player, but when Jack said them, it was an endearment. "Jack, could you do me one?" I asked.

"Anything," he said, and I knew he meant it.

"This Zachary Jones," I began. "Jack, the guy has admitted he was on the property the night Slim was killed. He insists he just showed up without an appointment, and when Stella wasn't available, he turned right around and left. I was wondering if the security footage might not have recorded his activities. Any way you might have time to take a look?"

"Huh," he said. "So he was here? I'll have a few minutes after I finish up reviewing the social director's agenda for tonight. Ring me back later."

"I have one stop to make then I'm crossing on the ferry. I'll see you soon, Bob," I said.

"Bob?" It took a minute. "Oh. Right. Bob Cratchit." He paused a few seconds before saying, "Why do I ever sign on for these things?"

I could hardly wait to see handsome Jack in his Bob Cratchit costume tonight at The Mansion's Ghostly Christmas Gala—and not only Jack. Several of my other friends would be appearing as characters from the Dickens classic.

After a couple of air kisses, we disconnected just as I arrived at St. Antoine's Children's Home.

My old friend and mentor, Father Brian, was shooting hoops in the courtyard with some of the boys. I sat down on a bench and watched. Brian was a good man. He was probably in his late forties. His shaggy hair had been grey since I'd first met him when I was graduating from high school. I loved him for his generous spirit, kind patience, and good humor.

After a few minutes, he looked over and saw me sitting there, and after dribbling the ball a few times, he bounced it over to one of the boys. "I'm gonna go talk to Melanie awhile," he said, "give you boys a little break."

He sat down beside me, his head turning as he watched the boys running circles under the hoop. "I heard about the terrible thing that happened at Mystic Isle on Tuesday. How grim. Did you know the man?"

I nodded. "Not all that well, but he seemed like a nice enough guy. He was funny. But I just learned that he wasn't all he seemed."

Father Brian shrugged. "Who of us really is?"

"He owed a lot of money to someone." I turned toward him. "A lot of money and to someone who might or might not be capable of killing him to get paid back by taking Papa Noël's gift bag."

Brian sat there a minute. "Did you hear that a bone marrow match has been found?"

"Really? That's great." But then I remembered all the money we collected to put toward Nicole's procedure was gone, taken from Slim's poor dead grip by some low-life, killer scum. Sure, I was being a bit dramatic, but when was drama called for if not now?

"The really bad thing about it is this woman's a missionary who's come forward and volunteered to donate, but she's leaving for her mission in Africa in a week."

I felt like crying but held it back. Father Brian was a sensitive soul and seemed to pick up on my emotions. He laid his hand on my shoulder.

"I just connect with these kids, you know." It was hard for me to talk about it. "They don't have anyone except you and the sisters."

"Well, and you and others who care about them."

"Yes, but they're not family. Not the kind of family a kid really needs. I had Mama, Grandmama Ida, and Granddaddy Joe. But I understand how vulnerable they must feel. When my father just up and left when I was five, even with Mama and my grandparents there to love me and support me, I felt like my world had turned upside down. I watched at the window for months, thinking he'd be coming home any day."

"These things are hard to understand." His voice was soft, kind.

"It's just due to that, I get how these kids must feel, on a smaller scale of course. I had more love when I was a kid than I knew what to do with. These boys and girls...they don't have that. And poor Nicole. She must be so scared and not have anyone to sit by her bed and..." I couldn't go on.

Father Brian seemed at a loss. "Sister Catherine is close to the child. We all do our best."

"I know you do, Father Brian. I just wish that money hadn't disappeared. She really needs it, especially now."

"We're making a plea to the congregation, but..." his voice trailed off.

"It doesn't look good?" I finished for him.

He shook his head, sending his unkempt hair falling down onto his forehead. His eyes were worried, a sentiment I shared with him.

"Man," I lamented. "I thought we had this covered. What kind of person would do that—kill Slim in the first place then take funds and gift cards intended for your kids?"

"Not a good person," he said. "And I want you to keep that in mind when you go running off trying to find the bag and get it back."

I just looked at him.

"Don't give me those big old innocent green eyes," he said seriously. "I know how you are, Melanie Hamilton. I also know it won't do any good to tell you not to try to track it down, so I'm just going to say a prayer you won't put yourself in danger to do it."

"A prayer, Father? How about if you say two?"

CHAPTER FOURTEEN

———

What Father Brian had said about poor Nicole felt like a bull elephant sitting on me. I couldn't breathe right, and my head spun with worry. The sweet little girl had been waiting for a blood marrow donor for over a year. In the meantime, her condition had grown worse and she'd grown weaker. We'd raised $70,000.00 in our holiday drive earmarked specifically to help defray the cost of her procedure should a suitable donor come along. And here we were with someone who matched, was willing and able, but who was also on a tight timetable—and no money.

I leaned over and told the cabbie, a Bobby DeNiro double, seventyish with the down-turned mouth and piercing dark eyes, "Please take me to the ferry dock by Café du Monde."

"You got it, girl."

Traffic was light on the freeway until we headed into the Quarter where holiday shoppers bustled around from store to store. When we neared the French Market, cars were stacked up like it was a parking lot, so I paid the hefty fare, got out, and walked the remaining few blocks.

I slipped off the jacket and stuffed it in my tote in case the bookie happened to be on the boat. Then I waited on the dock, watching the Mystic Isle ferry head back across. It was a flat-bottom ferry with a canopy. The canopy and sides were painted with fleur-de-lis and scrolls in Mardi Gras colors of purple, gold, and green. As it drew closer through the whirling water, I saw George, the conductor, leaning against the rail.

George had a mouth full of big ol' teeth that looked too large for his face when he grinned. His Adam's apple was so prominent I yearned to tease him about swallowing a Ping-Pong ball. But George was a really good guy with a heart of gold, and neither Cat nor I ever wanted to say anything that might hurt his feelings.

The ferry pulled up then sidled up beside the dock. George went straight to open the gate and put out the gangplank.

"Hey, Mel," George hollered when he saw me. "How you doin'?" He took my hand and helped me onto the gangplank. "I already ferried your counterpart across a while back."

"Cat's working," I told him. "It's my day off."

He gave me one of his endearing aw-shucks grins. "So you're probably crossing over just so's you get to talk to me. Ain't that right?" He winked.

"Absolutely, George. I just can't stand going even one day without talking shop with my favorite ferryman."

After about fifteen minutes, when no one else came, the ferry headed southeast cross-river to Algiers Point where, with any luck, the Mystic Isle shuttle bus was dropping off several departing guests for George to ferry back across.

It was a thirty-minute drive from the ferry landing to The Mansion at Mystic Isle, and I was the only passenger on the shuttle. The driver, a new guy I'd only met once before, tried to engage me in conversation, but I wasn't in the mood to chat—too preoccupied with Slim's murder, the theft of the bounty from our holiday charity drive, and what that might mean for Nicole's medical procedure if we couldn't find out who killed Slim and recover it.

He finally gave up, and we rode most of the way in silence. When he pulled the shuttle up under The Mansion's portico, I stepped down just in time to see Valentine Cantrell cross the threshold, where Lurch grabbed hold and lifted her off her feet in a big old bear hug while he snapped off a selfie.

When he set her back on her feet, he reached down and patted the top of her head affectionately like she was a wayward stray dog come back to the old homestead. Lurch was good people, odd people, but all the same good people.

"Valentine," I called out.

She turned around. I'd never seen her look as tired as she did just then. Her beautiful golden eyes were dull, her hair frizzy and unkempt.

"Hello, Mel," she said. She even sounded exhausted.

I hurried up the steps and across the veranda, where I wrapped my arms around her. "I'm so glad to see you," I said. "They let you go? That's wonderful."

She shook her head. "They didn't 'xactly 'let me go.' More like Harry posted bail. I'm still facing a court date in a couple of weeks, but at the hearing, the judge didn't deem me no flight risk, so I am coming back to work for as long as I can."

"Oh." That was disappointing news. I took hold of her hand. "Well, don't you worry, Val. I'm not going to rest until we figure out who killed poor Slim and took Papa Noël's bag. And we all know it wasn't you."

She smiled and nodded as tears welled in her eyes, and I could see she didn't trust herself to speak.

Valentine and I walked inside, and just as I was turning away to go find Jack and discuss whether or not he'd be able to help me do some gumshoeing...

"Hell's bells! I don't believe it!" It was Diane, Slim's wife, crossing the lobby. She grabbed hold of Valentine's arm and whipped her around.

Startled and maybe even a little frightened, Valentine drew back, yanking her arm away. "Mrs. Conner?" she said. "What is it?"

"Don't go and tell me they let you out of the slammer, you brazen man-stealing hussy!"

"I...I..." Valentine couldn't do anything but stutter. She looked around as if she was unsure what to do. And who could blame her?

Diane was on a rampage, grabbing Valentine's arm again. "Don't you think I didn't know you was shackin' up with my Slim? And don't you think he didn't tell me he was going to stop seeing you just to please me? And don't you think we all don't know you was probably so jealous-mad you ran him down just for spite?"

Valentine tried hard to loosen Diane's hold on her arm, but Diane hung on like a bulldog with a bone, going so far as to shake Valentine.

"Let go of me," Valentine said. "You're making a scene, and besides, I don't know what you're talking about. First of all, I wasn't 'shacking up' with poor Slim. He was a friend of mine, and he had some serious problems he didn't feel comfortable talking to anyone else about. Money problems. Gambling debts, if you want to know. He was worried about owing all that money. Woman, that man wasn't cheating on you as far as I know and f'sure not with me."

"You're lyin'," Diane screeched and grabbed Valentine's hair, jerking her head to one side.

Poor Valentine had no choice but to retaliate, lunging at Diane.

All heck broke loose then.

The two women went down on the floor, grappling. I felt sort of helpless and stupid and just stood there a minute watching them.

Someone up on the second floor landing who must have been looking down yelled. "Cat fight!"

Lurch, moving pretty darn fast for a Goliath over seven feet tall, leaned over and grabbed hold of both women and pulled them apart.

Diane stood there, struggling, heaving, and—I was pretty surprised—hissing at Valentine.

Valentine was crying. "What's wrong with you?"

I came to my senses, took hold of Val's hand, and pulled her outside with me, while Lurch stood passively, holding on to Diane almost tenderly, the whole time making a low disapproving sound in his throat.

I didn't look back to see what the outcome was going to be but instead propelled Valentine out the door, across the lawn, and over the property. She dug in her heels, stopping us outside the old boathouse on the dock.

She stood there a minute, tears flowing down her cheeks, her chest heaving with exertion and probably frustration and anxiety. "I just...I just..." She took a deep, ragged breath and let it out. "That woman is just plain old nuts."

I didn't add anything. In my opinion, that pretty much said it all.

At that moment, the door to the boathouse opened, and Odeo came out, carrying a big bag of fertilizer on each shoulder.

The minute he saw Valentine and me standing on the dock, he set them down and lumbered over to us.

By the sheer grief on his face and the shaking of his hands, it was obvious he was upset. "Oh, Miss Valentine," he moaned. "What is it's gone wrong with you? Why you cryin'?"

The very soul of patience and calm, Valentine took yet another deep breath then laid her hand on Odeo's muscular arm. "It's nothing, Odeo. Just pure spite that don't mean nothing really, and I'm just kind of tired is all."

At that point Odeo had worked himself into a fit and stood there shaking his head and shifting his weight side to side. "I knowed it," he whimpered. "I shoulda done what I meant to and told Chief Deputy Quincy it was me."

Both Valentine and I turned to stare at him.

"What do you mean it was you?" I asked.

"Well, Miss Melanie, if I had said it was me all along, none of this trouble would've landed at Valentine's feet. They would've taken me, not her."

Valentine's voice was so soft I could barely hear her. Her hand stayed where it was on Odeo's arm, but her fingers curled a little tighter. "Are you sayin' it was you killed Slim Conner?" She couldn't hide the fear and shock in her voice. "Tell me it wasn't you, Odeo."

I held my breath.

He looked down at her. "If I said I did, maybe things'd be better for you. I love you, Miss Valentine, and I hate it that they's all giving you so much trouble."

You could have shoveled my jaw up off the dock, and that set Valentine and me both to crying.

He went on. "I'm a gonna do it. I'll be telling Deputy Q it was me all along, and they gonna be letting you get on back to your life."

Val shook her head. "You can't do that, Odeo. Not if it wasn't you."

I remembered what he'd said on the bus, about how he'd hurt Slim, and all I could think was how big he was, and how easily it was to upset him, and that a man as simple as Odeo could easily have done something in a fit of rage he might not even have remembered doing.

CHAPTER FIFTEEN

―――

We never got a straight answer from Odeo as to whether or not he'd actually been the person who ran over Slim Conner with the utility van, but we did manage to convince him not to go running to the Sheriff with some crazy kind of confession just to save Valentine. I was having a hard time believing he could be cruel or vicious. And even more trouble believing if he'd killed Papa Noël in an act of passion over the issue of the purloined liquor that he would have taken the bag of holiday goodies well known to have been intended for the orphans.

I walked Valentine around the building to the side entrance then into the kitchen. Everyone turned when we came in. A cheer went up, and we were immediately surrounded by the ten kitchen workers who made up the day staff.

There were smiles, laughter, and even some tears. Only Aaron stood back, but by the look of relief on his face, I could tell he was as happy as everyone else to see her.

Valentine stood and accepted the hugs and well wishes of her staff for a moment, and then she wiped her eyes with the back of her hand. "All right, people, thank you for such a spirited welcome, but let's get back to it." She crossed the room and removed a freshly laundered chef's jacket from a cabinet, donned it over her T-shirt, and buttoned it, leaving the top button loose.

Aaron came up to us and handed me a plate with an egg salad sandwich and a scoop of coleslaw. "Take a load off, Mel. And thanks for bringing her back to us," he said. "She was missed."

The sandwich, piled high with The Mansion's Cajun egg salad on a hoagie roll, looked delish. "I didn't bring her back. Mr. Villars paid her bail. I just walked in with her." I hadn't had anything solid to eat since early that morning, and I didn't hesitate to sit down in the corner away from the food prep area. "She's still charged, Aaron. The real killer's still out there somewhere, and we still have to convince the sheriff's office it wasn't Valentine." I couldn't help thinking of Odeo.

Valentine stopped at the sink and spent more than a couple of minutes scrubbing her hands then came back to me, still drying them on a paper towel. "But you did keep me from clawing that Conner woman's eyes out, and *I* wanna thank you for that."

Aaron looked back and forth between us, but Valentine just smiled at him and moved over to a counter where she opened a laptop and began to scroll through menu options.

"She's just a special person, isn't she?" Aaron said.

My mouth was full of sandwich, so instead of even trying to answer, I just nodded.

He stood looking at me a minute, and rather than let all that goodness go to waste, I took another huge bite out of the sandwich. He went on. "What can I do to help you? We need to get her out of harm's way. It just kills me that such a good person has to go through this."

I swallowed hard then answered. "Listen, Aaron, if you really mean it. I can use all the help I can get. I don't want them to pin this on her any more than any of you do." I swept the room with my hand, er, make that my sandwich. "We all love her."

"Well, I mean it," he said. "Just tell me how I can help."

I hadn't considered asking him specifically for help investigating the case, but the minute he'd offered, an idea popped into my head. "You're a good-looking guy," I said.

He didn't look surprised when I said it, even if the timing of such a bold-faced remark was odd. A guy like that probably had women panting around him all the time, which brought me to—"Do you think you might cozy up to Slim's wife?"

He looked at me for a minute, obviously trying to work out what I was getting at. I hurried to explain. "She was badmouthing Val and is one of the main reasons Chief Deputy Boudreaux arrested Valentine, that and Val's fingerprints on the van."

"Yeah." His voice was low, his tone dark and sad. "And don't forget the blood and mud all over her rain boots."

"Diane put it in Quincy's head that Valentine was having some sort of clandestine affair with her husband, and because he wanted to end it, Val killed him."

"She said that?" He shook his head. "Doesn't make sense, does it? A woman like Chef Valentine with a loser like Slim Conner."

"No, it doesn't, and Valentine already said she was just friends with Slim."

"Just friends?" He seemed to be struggling to put it together. "So you think Diane lied to the deputies?"

"I don't know if she lied exactly. I think she believed it, maybe even believed it enough to kill her husband in a jealous rage. If you could somehow get Diane talking about it, maybe she'd make a mistake and let something slip."

"But why me?"

"Why not? You said you wanted to help. The only other guy I can think of who might be able to charm her enough to make her loose-tongued is Jack Stockton."

"The hotel manager, right?"

"Right. And he's busy with holiday events right now." *And besides, I don't want my Cap'n Jack cozying up to any woman, not even one as, IMHO, unappealing as Diane Conner.*

Aaron pressed his lips into a hard line. "All right," he said. "I'll do it. I just have to figure out a way how." He pulled a napkin across the table and a pen from his pocket, pausing to jot something on the napkin. He handed it to me. "Here's my phone number and address. I don't live far from here or from Valentine either if that helps. So if you need me for anything else..."

I looked down. "Sure," I said. "Thanks."

I left the kitchen, confident that Aaron would help me move my investigation forward.

Jack wasn't in his office where he'd normally be at two thirty on a Thursday afternoon. His assistant said he'd received a phone call about something going on over in the plantation cemetery and had "...taken off outta here like somebody lit a fire under him."

The old cemetery was located at the rear of the property, just away from the public areas. It took me about ten minutes to walk over there.

I stopped on the crest of the hill, looking down at what was normally a serene and lovely scene of the area that was surrounded by willows and strewn with ancient stone markers.

But not today.

All the action was going on in the dead center, pun intended, around a particularly large gravestone.

The stone itself was about three feet tall and wide, and half again as deep. Perched on top of it was a statue of Eugenia Villars, one of Harry Villars' ancestors who died way back in 1823. A five-point star inside a circle was engraved above her name and the date of her death. Eugenia, I'd learned from my mandatory study of The Mansion's history, was a pagan and nature worshiper of great renown who'd lashed herself to an enormous willow in an effort to discourage her father from burning the grove to cultivate more land for cotton. The annals of history reveal she was brave and passionate but not very bright because not only was the tree she lashed herself to in the deepest, darkest middle of the grove where no one could see her, but she forgot to mention her protest to anyone, and when the fires were set, no one knew she was there, and she succumbed to the fire.

The Ravens evidently loved her for her sacrifice, as they were cavorting and carrying on, circling her grave like Ring-Around-the-Rosie. I stood there, the afternoon sun shining in my eyes, watching the Ravens celebrate, trying to figure out why Jack would have been so alarmed that he'd run out here.

When I put a hand over my brow to shade my eyes from sun—well, I got it. I really got it. About half the Ravens, some men, some women, were nude, and every time they made another circle around the grave, yet another one would stop and shuck off his clothes. Long branches with what looked like mistletoe were then held over his or her head, and all the Ravens took turns laying a big old juicy kiss on the newly disrobed individual before the circling began again.

Poor Jack ran frantically from place to place, picking up the robes off the ground and pleading with the Ravens to take them from him and put them on. His frantic voice carried up the hill on the chill breeze. "Please, please, people. This just isn't...isn't...what management had in mind when we encouraged you to celebrate the holidays in your own way."

It only took another minute or two for the rest of them to get naked. Poor Jack finally gave up, opened his arms, let all the robes fall back to the yellowed grass, and turned around. That was when he noticed me. He lifted his arms in a what-the-heck-can-I-do gesture and began to trudge back up the hill.

When he joined me, he put one arm around my shoulder and placed his other hand over my eyes, blocking the view, which had begun to get a little out of hand with all the mistletoe being passed around.

"I'm hoping they'll get cold pretty soon and give it up," he said.

That made me laugh as he turned me around and began to head back toward the main building.

"What are you doing out here anyway?" he asked.

"Valentine's back," I said. "I thought you'd want to know."

"Thank God," he said with a sigh of relief. "Maybe things'll settle down some."

I laughed again. "Only if you get her to put catnip in the Ravens' food." I stopped, and since we were holding hands, he stopped too. "Did you have a chance yet to look at the security video?"

"I did. And there is footage of Zachary Jones at the resort the night of the murder. The cameras caught him heading into the resort then later across the lawn to the boathouse."

"The boathouse?" My heart beat faster. "Where the utility van that ran down Slim had been parked for the evening."

CHAPTER SIXTEEN

———

I spent an hour cleaning and organizing Dungeons and Deities for the next day's busy schedule. I had a set of middle-aged triplets, men, lined up for the day and wanted to be prepared in case they decided the three separate Hear No Evil, See No Evil, Speak No Evil monkey tattoos I'd already designed for them weren't elaborate enough. I'd spent a lot of time on them, and they'd turned out so well I was thinking of offering the men a discounted price if they'd agree to let me incorporate the designs into my portfolio.

After that, I headed for the employee's locker room where The Mansion's social director had texted all costumes for the evening had been delivered. They had. The silly thing I had to wear made me cringe. It consisted of a Christmas plaid dress with a fitted bodice and enormous full-length bell skirt, over it, a furry white capelet, and then a bonnet worthy of a Jane Austen heroine. Grandmama Ida had a porcelain bell in her china cabinet handed down a couple of generations. It was a small woman whose torso was the handle with a clapper that moved freely inside the enormous skirt. When I looked in the mirror, I felt like its twin. Not exactly my style.

I was one of the few female employees, aside from serving staff, who'd agreed to attend tonight. I did it because of Jack, because he'd been worried that due to the *A Christmas Carol* theme, there wouldn't be enough costumed women at the event. I found myself doing lots of things because of Jack these days, and I liked it.

Jack was just crossing the lobby when I emerged from behind the grand staircase to the second floor. The swish of my silly skirt and jingle bells on the ties of the capelet made everyone in the lobby stop and turn, including Jack—who, BTW, looked adorable.

His Bob Cratchit outfit consisted of a threadbare brown wool jacket over a dull brown vest and slacks. The white high-collared shirt had ruffled cuffs that peeked out from the jacket sleeves and was anchored by a black string tie. His knee-high boots didn't look like poor old Bob Cratchit could have afforded them, but they hugged his calves and set off his muscular thighs just so. A fairly tattered top hat sat tilted back on his head.

Too cute.

"Why, Miss Hamilton." He was trying to sound like Bob Cratchit, too, but it came out more like Sir Paul McCartney than Sir Patrick Stewart. "You look more Christmassy than a plum pudding."

He offered me the crook of his arm, and we entered the Ghostly Christmas Gala.

The main salon had been made over into a Victorian era London street, complete with cardboard facades of quaint shops and buildings and fake polymer snow hauled in on order of Harry Villars.

The room was alive with charm. Old Marley, the Ghost of Christmas Past, née Lurch, dragged this chains around the salon, dust, née Johnson's Baby Powder from the scent of it, floating off his shredded garb as he moved. His deep and miserable moan was pretty scary and would have frightened children if there had been any in attendance.

Odeo, the Ghost of Christmas Yet-to-Come, lumbered the room as the grim reaper, sickle and all. His face and dark skin sunken back into the cowl made the place where his features should have been look eerily like a black hole.

Fabrizio, the Ghost of Christmas Present, was the very spirit of Christmas in bright furry robes. Harry as Ebenezer Scrooge was appropriately dour. And Melvin, the little person who'd performed Lurch's Christmas elf counterpart so beautifully the night Slim was murdered, made a fine Tiny Tim, crutch under one arm, knickers, and knee socks.

He hobbled over when we walked in and glared up at Jack. "I go out to the levee with you and knock a few heads together on your behalf, and this is the thanks I get? What the heck? Tiny Tim? I mean, could we be any more cliché here?"

Jack looked truly repentant. "Hey, Melvin, believe me." He ran one hand from his own head downward. "None of this was my idea. Tonight, we play the roles we're assigned."

Melvin snorted. "Still. I mean, really?" and hobbled away.

"Not a happy Tiny Tim, is he?" I said."

"Hm-mm." Jack said. "Man, I hope he doesn't hit anybody with that crutch."

I looked around just in time to see Diane walk into the main salon, looking like a little lost lamb, make that a lost bulldog. Her expression couldn't have been described any other way except surly. It was any wonder Slim, every bit as jolly as Papa Noël himself, had anything to do with her.

She made her way over to the bar, where one of the female bartenders who normally worked the Presto-Change-o Room and Aaron Bronson, on loan from the kitchen staff, tended bar. In matching costumes, they looked like they belonged together on a shelf—Mr. and Mrs. Royal Doulton Dickensian Figurines. She in a corseted white blouse and red skirt—he in a white long-sleeved shirt with a black bow tie and black sleeve garters under a red vest. Both wore white aprons.

"Jack, I'm going to see if Aaron needs a break."

Jack looked up, saw Aaron behind the bar, saw Diane sitting down in front of the bar, and, smart as a whip, made the connection.

He placed his hand briefly on my shoulder, moving his fingers back and forth. "Good luck."

I lifted the bar gate and joined Aaron who was filling a pilsner glass with draft beer. "Hello, Mel." His eyes never left the glass, which he topped off before turning to me.

With a lift of my chin and a shift of my eyes, I directed his attention to where Diane sat at the far end of the bar. He nodded and lifted the pilsner glass. "She likes her draft," he said.

"You know, Aaron, if you wanted to take a little break and spend some time getting to know the guests..."

His eyes opened wide. "Oh," he said. "Right. But I'm supposed to—"

"I don't mind covering back here."

He looked doubtful, but I hurried to say, "I did a little bartending in my college days." It was a complete lie, but I wanted him to be relaxed and comfortable while he fished for information. And besides, how hard could it be?

He untied his apron, helped me into it, and moved around behind me, tying it before picking up the beer he'd just poured and heading out and around the bar to where Diane sat.

He spoke to her, and while I could hear his voice, I couldn't distinguish what he said. She looked up at him as he set down the beer, and her smile transformed her face.

She said something back.

They were too far away for me to overhear. *Dang it!* I couldn't stand it.

Aha! Bar mix! Keeping my head down and my face half-hidden by the brim of the bonnet, I picked up the bowl, waddled over—my hoop skirt swinging around me like my legs were the clapper on a big old bell—and set the bowl in front of them then turned my back, hanging close by.

"I remember you from the dinner party Sunday night," Aaron began. "Mrs. Conner, right?"

"You must have a mind for names?" she said, her inflection lifting at the end of the sentence, her tone actually kind of sweet. I couldn't stand not seeing them, so I turned back around but kept my head down.

She took a long pull from the glass, wiping the foam off her lip with the back of her hand like a dockworker before laying her hand back on top of the bar. Aaron covered her hand with his then removed it and wiped it on his shirtsleeve. His face never changed, the smile still plastered on his face.

"My condolences on the death of your husband," Aaron said.

She ducked her head. "Thank you."

There was a lull in the conversation, and I briefly had to wonder if I'd put the wrong man on the assignment. But Aaron was just getting started. His hand was back on hers. "You must miss him."

With her free hand, she took another pull on the beer, the foam lining her upper lip before her tongue slipped out and slithered over it. "Not really," she said with no girlish inflection this time. "If I'm being honest, he wasn't much of a husband when it came right down to it."

"Oh?" This time it was Aaron's turn to question.

"Hey, Red!"

I looked down the bar where a man sat, waving in my direction.

"Mix me up a hurricane, will ya?" he hollered.

"Really?" I hollered back. "You sure you wouldn't like a nice cold beer or a glass of wine?"

"Nope, it's a hurricane for me all right."

I recognized the troublemaker from earlier today. He'd been one of the naked fools dancing around the gravestone. Now, there was something I didn't think I'd ever be able to unsee.

Without moving too far from where Aaron and Diane sat, I reached up and took down one of our souvenir hurricane glasses from the backbar, opened the spiral notebook with the mixed drink recipes, and began to move around, searching for the ingredients. My ears were still peaked to the conversation between Diane and Aaron.

Diane was expounding on poor Slim's shortcomings. "I wanted kids, you know. A whole parcel of 'em. But nooooo. Slim wouldn't have it. And I even tried to trick him into it a couple of times. You know, dim lights, his favorite banjo pickin' music, a few cold frosty ones? He'd just dance around to the tunes, drink the beers, and pass out. That louse never even tried to keep it from me that he was seein' that hussy? Can you imagine?"

"Which hussy would that be?" Aaron, diplomatic to the end.

"Why, Miss Valentine You-Better-Keep-an-Eye-on-Your-Husbands Cantrell. That's who." Diane slammed the empty pilsner glass back on the bar and yelled, "Bring me another Miller." She took a second to look Aaron over, starting at his face, her eyes moving lower before, "Make that a Miller Lite, will ya?"

I was going back and forth between the hurricane and the interrogation. One ounce light rum. One ounce dark rum. One ounce...

I stopped and drafted Diane a fresh beer then carried it over, head down. But I didn't have to worry. She never looked up at me. Aaron was leaning an elbow on the bar, his head resting on his hand, his smile—even as stuck as I was on Cap'n Jack—was great.

"So, you and Slim were having problems? You poor thing." With his free hand he reached up and squeezed her shoulder.

I prayed neither Valentine nor Harry would choose that moment to walk in and see one of the staff manhandling one of the guests, whether she was a paying guest or not. It wasn't appropriate. But I didn't care. I was desperate to find someone to draw the police away from Valentine. I didn't want it to be Odeo, and I didn't know for sure if it was Zachary. And if it turned out to be Diane, I wouldn't shed any tears over it.

"Oh, yeah," she said. "He was carrying on with that Cantrell woman."

Had I added all three types of rum? Or just the one? I started over just to be sure.

Aaron seemed reluctant to say it, but he finally agreed. "I've heard that too."

Diane's eyes opened wide. "You've heard it too? Well, I've seen it with my own two eyes. Him and her a'hugging it out in the parking lot one night when I came to pick him up. Shameful."

"You saw them?" Aaron said.

"I did." And even though my back was turned as I fussed over my hurricane concoction, I knew she was finishing off her second beer from the glugging sounds she made and the way the glass sounded when it hit the bar. "I could've just killed that bastard."

Aaron's voice was low but even. "Did you?"
Diane's was suddenly shrill. "Did I what?"
"Kill him?"
She dismissed him with a wave of her hand. "Don't be silly."

I strained the hurricane over the crushed ice into the glass, picked it up, and carried it over to the Raven. It smelled a little strong to me, but then I wasn't much of a drinker, so what did I know?

"'Bout darn time." He grabbed the glass, took out the straw and the fruit, and turned up the glass, immediately choking and coughing.

OMG! I thought he might fall off his stool for a minute. All I needed was to get fired over poisoning one of the hotel guests. Especially one of the Ravens.

But I didn't need to worry after all. His flattened palm hit the bar. "Holy Jupiter, Red! You mix one helluva drink."

I looked back down the length of the bar. Aaron was alone.

"Well, crud," I said. As skillful and charming as Aaron had been, she hadn't given us any more to go on than we had before.

Aaron came back and took over the bar duties, while I walked out into the main salon, where it seemed Jack's worst fears had come to fruition.

Marvin, née Tiny Tim, was in a heated discussion with a man who was over six feet tall and must have weighed three hundred pounds. Their voices rose over the rest of the noise in the room, and people were turning to stare. Jack, née Bob Cratchit, broke away from the guests he was schmoozing just in time to hustle Marvin away, while Fabrizio, the Ghost of Christmas Present, joined the angry guest, handing him a cup of eggnog and engaging him in a conversation.

Marvin, carrying his forgotten crutch, stomped over to the bar and laid down a ten-spot. "Bourbon," he demanded. "A double. Straight up."

I looked across the room at Jack, who shrugged and nodded, so I located a bottle of Maker's Mark and poured him three ounces.

Marvin grabbed it, took one healthy swig, and saluted me with the glass. "Thanks, Mel. This'll make this freaky gig a bit more palatable."

Tiny Tim crutched his way back across the room, stopping every few feet to sip his bourbon.

Somewhere in my head, I thought I heard my Granddaddy Joe, the man who'd raised me and whose passing I still mourned, say, "Take my word for it, Mellie gal. My old pal Charles Dickens just rolled over in his grave. I saw him do it."

CHAPTER SEVENTEEN

———

It was early Friday morning. I'd stayed over with Jack in his "honeymoon cottage."

When I woke up, the spot beside me in bed was empty but still warm. I found him in the kitchenette, already dressed and on the phone.

I glanced at the heart-shaped clock on the wall. Six thirty. The sky through the kitchen window was just barely beginning to grey. The central heat kicked on, and I knew it would be a cold December day at The Mansion.

This wasn't the first time I'd slept over with Jack—even if we never did much actual sleeping—so I was familiar with the kitchenette and where he kept everything, including the K-Cups. Lately, he'd always stocked my favorite Coffee & Chicory pods. What a man.

While he talked, I fixed his coffee, black, and handed it to him. My guess was he was on a long-distance call with the travel agent in Dublin who was sending us a group of sixty guests in March. He lifted his cup, showing his appreciation.

"We've lined up the speakers and entertainers you requested on the subjects of banshees and leprechauns. Our normal staff of magicians, mediums, tarot readers, and so on will be available to your group as well."

Next, I fixed my own coffee—I liked it *regulah*, as we like to say in the Big Easy, with lots of cream and a ton of sugar. Mm-hmm. The best way to start any morning.

I sat down at the small table with Jack.

He rubbed my bare knee sticking out from under one of his T-shirts. His fingers were warm from when he'd held the coffee mug. I laid my hand on his and squeezed. My feelings for

Jack were strong—fondness, admiration, and passion. Lately, he'd also become my safe haven. He'd been there for me when Fabrizio had been accused of murder, and I'd been frantic to help him. And more and more, I found myself relying on his solid judgment when I needed advice.

I'd seen him deal with irate guests with patience and kindness, eventually disarming them with his utter charm. And I'd seen him deal with employees from high-dollar entertainers to janitors with equal respect. He was good at his job not only because of his training and experience but mainly because of his people skills and true caring nature.

And he was a great lover, who made me feel safe and confident, and could always make me laugh.

Love was a strong word, and one I'd never used before when relating to a man, but it was a word that came to mind when I thought of Jack Stockton. My Cap'n Jack.

I got up, set my cup in the sink, and made a motion to him of rubbing my hands over my face and under my arms.

"One second, please," he said into the phone and lowered it. "I'll probably be gone when you get out of the shower. Couple of more calls to make. How about meeting me for breakfast in the employee lounge in about an hour?"

I nodded and went into the bathroom, turned on the shower, and stepped in.

After my shower, I made my way to the main building. It was cold outside, but the walk wasn't a long one.

My first appointment wasn't until nine thirty, the triplets with the monkeys, so before changing into my costume, I stopped in at the employee lounge where Jack and I planned to meet for a quick breakfast.

Valentine Cantrell sat nursing a cup of tea at one of the tables. Her long, elegant fingers ran over the handle of the cup. Even sitting down, she was as graceful as a ballet dancer.

"Mornin', Mel." Her low, sultry voice and laid-back style always calmed me. "Time for breaking that fast." She shoved a plate full of fragrant cinnamon buns in my direction. The pastries were thick with cream cheese frosting and so spiced with sweet cinnamon, you could taste them long after they'd been chewed and swallowed.

Even though I tried restraint, I nearly launched myself at the plate. This wasn't my first Valentine Cantrell Sinful Cinnamon Roll. *And, dear Lord, don't let it be my last.*

I bit into it and chewed, trying hard to keep the saliva from dripping out of my mouth. "I see you're back in full force." I gave her a thumbs up.

She sighed, circling her tea mug with both hands. "I'm so grateful Louise covered for me. And she did a darn fine job of it too. Don't have even the faintest idea how things would have gone without her."

I waited. From her tone, I knew more was coming.

It came. "But I can't find hardly even a single thing in that big old kitchen. It's like someone came through and just waved a magic wand, and everything switched itself around."

"Really?" I said. "Louise reorganized your kitchen in just one day?"

Val shrugged. "Either that or I went senile sitting in that jail."

Sobering thought. Valentine Cantrell in lockup? "Was it terrible?"

"Oh, sweet girl. Not so bad. I had the place all to myself pretty much, and people kept coming in to check on me. They were downright accommodating. But I missed my boy something awful."

"I know you did." There wasn't much left to say except, "We're trying to help figure out who the real killer is so you don't have to go back there. It just broke my heart thinking about you in that place."

"Are you maligning the outstanding facility provided by the good taxpayers of Jefferson Parish?"

We both looked up.

It was Quincy.

I thought I saw something that might be labeled fear flash briefly in Valentine's golden eyes. But it was gone in an instant. "Why if it isn't Chief Deputy Boudreaux." She got to her feet and went to the counter. "Let me get you a cuppa Joe, child."

"No, thank you, Valentine. I'm here on department business. There's been a development."

"Oh?" was all she said, but her hand found mine and latched on. I curled my fingers around hers.

It was obvious by the concerned look on Quincy's face, the development he'd mentioned wasn't going to be good news.

And it wasn't.

"For the sake of due diligence, we been checkin' into a few things, Chef Cantrell."

She didn't speak, but her eyes begged him not to go any further. I couldn't blame her for being worried about the news he was about to deliver.

He was doing his best to sound casual. "The folks over at the Childress Music Academy, don't ya know, they been tellin' us 'bout this little miracle. Seems like out of a clear blue sky somebody up and paid $65,000.00 so your boy, Benjy, can become a piano virtuoso. An anonymous cash delivery was added to Benjy's account on Wednesday, the day after the murder, the day after the donations were stolen." He let it hang there a bit before, "You wouldn't happen to know anything 'bout that, now. Would you, Chef Cantrell?"

"You said what now?" Valentine let go of my hand and stood. "I have no earthly idea where that kind of money would come from all in one chunk. Last I heard they were working on setting up a payment plan for me, and that was gonna be a stretch. Since you been *checkin'*..." Her emphasis made checking sound more like snooping. "...I'm sure you're just all over my $58,000.00 a year salary. And I'm betting you even know I won't be coming up for salary review for a few more months yet."

He didn't speak, but his brown eyes were alert.

Valentine went on. "So you comin' on in here and getting' all up in my face 'bout where did that $65,000.00 come from is just a load of..." She stopped. "Well, it just don't make much sense." She sat back down and drummed her fingers on the tabletop.

Quincy scratched his chin, twisted his head, swung a chair around backwards, and straddled it. "I take that to mean you weren't the one providing all that largesse to the academy then?"

Valentine's dander was still up. "What do you think, Chief Deputy? No. Wait. Let me guess. You think I snagged the key to one of the resort vans, snuck out to the boathouse, drove out along the service road, ran over my good friend Slim Conner, rounded back for a second go at him, climbed out of the van in the pouring rain, stole all those donations for those sweet little orphans and all the money for that poor sick little girl, and then sent it over to the music school just so as my Benjy, who's already a genius at playin' piano, can leave his mother's lovin' arms and stay all the way across the river to take lessons in music theory and technique from folks who just might know less about it than the boy does already? Humph. Does that make sense to you, Chief Deputy?"

Quincy had the grace to shrug.

On a roll, she asked again, "Well, does it?"

"Not completely, no," he said. "Look, Valentine." His voice went soft. "I'd be just pleased as could be if it was to come out it was somebody else who did in Papa Noël and stole his bag o' goodies. But so far, all the evidence is pointin' toward you. We really don't have anything leadin' us to believe someone else would have done it. Mrs. Conner has done said you were knockin' boots with her husband—"

"Well, that's a damn lie," Valentine shrieked.

"—and then we got your prints, and the boots, and you can't really account for where you were." He sighed. "And now this here big money shows up at the school. What else are we supposed to think?"

She leaned back in her chair, seeming to shrink before my eyes. "Looks like my goose might be sitting in a 325-degree oven, just waiting to get basted and served."

"Not so fast," I said. "Have you and your people even considered looking at anyone else?"

"You mean like Odeo Fournet?" Quincy asked.

Oops. That wasn't what I had in mind—hadn't been looking to get another one of my friends in trouble, and I didn't believe he'd been the one to kill Slim, anyway. No more than I believed Valentine had done it.

"Well, not Odeo. But what about Diane Conner? She looks pretty guilty to me. Didn't like her husband, and not only did she have some crazy idea that Slim was having an affair with Valentine—a pretty darn good motive if you ask me, a woman scorned and all that. But she also knew he was gambling away all their money. And now that we're talking about gambling, have you taken a good look at Zachary Jones?"

Quincy frowned. "Who?"

"Zachary Jones," I blurted out. "The bookie Slim owed all that money to. I mean, come on, Quincy. Don't those kind of people give you cement sneakers if you don't pay up on time, or nail your knees to the floor, or something?"

Quincy just sat there, looking at me. "Melanie Hamilton, you been digging into this investigation?"

Uh-oh.

He went on. "Like you done last time? Like I asked you not to do this time?"

I swallowed hard.

He sat there a minute longer, just staring at me then he ran his fingers through his hair, which was already standing straight up. "Looks like maybe I better hear all about this fella, Zachary Jones."

So I told him what I knew. He just sat there, rubbing his hand along his jaw, listening like it was story hour at the library.

"Hey, if it isn't Chief Deputy Quincy Boudreaux, Cajun gentleman extraordinaire!" Cap'n Jack walked into the room. "What a coincidence. Just the man I needed to see."

Quincy turned away from me. "Good morning, Jack. I was hoping to see you too."

"Everything all set?" Jack asked.

Huh? My head turned back to Quincy.

"You bet it is," he said. "But I'm scared right out of my socks."

What were these two cooking up?

Jack clapped him on the shoulder. "No worries, man. It'll come off like buttah."

Quincy gulped and nodded, but neither of them offered to let me in on the secret. I planned to grill Jack the earliest chance I had.

Jack went on. "Anything new on those thefts we've been having?"

Quincy shook his head. "Nothing that will help us anyway. We still think it's an inside job. Whoever is pulling them off knows how to avoid the security cameras, when the rooms are empty, and how to get in and out without breaking the locks or being seen."

"I know it's probably occurred to you there hasn't been another incident since Tuesday," Jack said.

Quincy nodded. "Yeah. It has."

"And are you thinking it's connected to Santa— I mean Papa Noël's—bag being taken?"

One side of Quincy's mouth turned up. "Well, of course, Jack. What do you think? Just because we out here in the bayou we got heads full o' cotton?"

"No, no." Jack hurried to say. "Of course not. I know the deputies are on the job. I know you're one heck of an investigator. I'm not. Just because I thought it might all be connected…what do I know? It might not make any sense to someone who actually knows what he's doing. That's why I ran it by you."

Quincy punched Jack's arm. "Chill out, city boy. I was just pushing your button."

"Right," Jack said with a little laugh. "One of these days, I'll figure out all the nuances of Louisiana humor."

He walked over to the counter, fixed himself a cup of coffee, and then joined the three of us at the table, snagging one of Valentine's warm, gooey cinnamon rolls.

His eyes rolled up while he chewed his first bite. With the roll held in one hand, he pointed a finger of his other hand at it while he swallowed. "Valentine Cantrell. You're a genius and one of the main reasons I'm glad I came to work here."

She waved him off. "You go on."

He turned and winked at me.

Quincy sat there another moment before reaching over and grabbing not one but two of Valentine's pastries. "You know what? I'm thinking those pastries might require a bit of investigation, after all." Half of one was gobbled up in just one bite.

CHAPTER EIGHTEEN

———

After Quincy left, Valentine got to her feet. "Better get back. The kitchen'll be humming with breakfast orders, and I need to set up the lunch menu."

"Try not to worry, Valentine," I said. "Jack and I are still trying to figure this whole thing out, and now it sounds like even Quincy is looking around for another suspect."

She smiled and nodded then left the room.

Jack reached for another roll, while I scooted my chair closer to his. "What's going on with you and Quincy and the sly looks you keep giving each other?"

Jack chewed and opened his eyes wide, but I wasn't buying it. "I know you, Jack Stockton, and I know Quincy Boudreaux, and the two of you got something up your sleeves. I wanna know what it is."

He shook his head and swallowed. "I don't know what you're talking about." But he knew what I was talking about, and he knew I knew he knew what I was talking about.

"Okay. Fine," I said, standing. "If that's the way it's gonna be, I'll just have to get Cat to worm it out of Quincy."

He stood too, using his thumb to wipe a smudge of cream cheese frosting off my cheek and lick it off his finger. "Good luck with that," was all he said.

It was hot, but I stood my ground, not letting him distract me. "We'll see."

If Jack wouldn't crack, surely Quincy would.

I went back to the employee locker room and dressed in my costume—I liked to call it *Transylvania chic*.

As I crossed the lobby to head to the auxiliary wing and my tattoo parlor, Dragons and Deities, Diane Conner was heading toward the exit.

She stopped dead when she saw me. "What in blazes are you dressed up for?"

"Oh," I said. "It's just my work costume. We all wear them. You know, like the wizard's robe Slim wore when he was tending bar?"

"What?"

"Wizard's robes. All the bartenders wear them."

"That nice young man from the other night wasn't wearing any stupid wizard robe."

"Well, yeah. But that was a special event. We all dressed up like Dickens characters."

"Like who?"

"It was just something different."

She stood there a minute, chewing gum—chewing it loudly. "You telling me this place had Slim dress up like some kind of Merlin or something?"

I nodded.

"Well, isn't that just a crock?"

I shrugged, kind of stumped. "You never saw him in costume?"

She shook her head.

"Too bad," I said. "He wore the robe with panache."

"Pan-what?"

"He looked good in them."

"Figures," she said. "If I'd known more about him before we got hitched, I probably would have passed." She glanced at the medieval-looking clock on the wall behind the reception desk. It was one of those big wood and antique brass jobs with the works exposed in the middle and roman numerals to mark the hours, something you'd have expected to see in a dusty old museum. The way the exposed cogs and wheels moved had always fascinated me. But the most important thing about it was that it kept accurate time. "Well, I gotta boogie. Slim's ashes gotta be picked up."

"Oh." I instantly forgave her all the briskness and sarcasm. "I'm so sorry."

"Why are you sorry?" she said. "I should've known as big a hassle as that man was in life, he'd still be an inconvenience in death." She sighed. "But God help me. I did love him."

"Of course," I said.

"Too bad he was a liar and a cheater and gambled away all our money."

What could I say?

As it turned out, I didn't need to say anything. She had more to say. "You know he was sneaking around on me with that Creole woman, don't you?"

I began, "I don't—"

But she cut me off. "Sinful. That's what it is. All them war widows are just alike. Think they're entitled, that's what. Think just because their soldiers died defending this country, it makes them some kind o' special."

"What in the blue blazes are you talking about? Military wives make huge sacrifices. They are special and war widows even more so. Why would you say that about them in general and Valentine in particular?"

She lifted her chin defiantly. "Well, it's true. Isn't it? What kind of woman is that Valentine person? Carrying on like that, running around with a married man in broad daylight and in front of your own young child. Woman like that doesn't even deserve to have a child." She was so bitter it was like there were toxic fumes rising off her.

I turned, wanting to get away from her as quickly as possible. Who needed that negative energy? Certainly not me. Then I remembered. "Don't forget we're having that memorial service for Slim in the garden this afternoon."

"Huh," she said. "Won't be seeing me there. I'll be handling things my own way, if you please. Heading over to the city to sprinkle his ashes at the Harrah's casino, seeing as how he thought that place was more his home than the one I made for him."

"I see." But I didn't. I didn't have a clue how a person like Diane got to be that way.

"You wouldn't be trying to sneak away without paying me, would you?"

I spun around.

Zachary Jones had walked up behind us. He took hold of Diane's arm just above the elbow.

She tried to jerk away, but he held on.

"You know your deadbeat husband owed me a pretty penny, and the jerk stiffed me out of it all. So, I'm going to be looking to you to make good on it."

Diane began to shake and whimper, her gaze shifting to beg me for help. "Don't let him hurt me. Call the police."

We all three turned as one as Lurch's low moan rumbled around us.

Zachary let go of Diane like she was a hot potato. He stepped away. "No need to call the police." He was nervous and understandably so. I'd probably have been nervous too if I ran an illegal gambling parlor. He began to move away toward the auxiliary wing where Stella by Starlight plied her wares. But he stopped and looked around. "I'll be in touch, Mrs. Conner. Don't forget. I know where you live." He paused another minute, his gaze turning to me. "You look familiar. Do I know you from somewhere else?" He squinted.

My heart jumped up into my throat. At least it felt that way. "Well, yeah," I said quickly. "I was in the Presto-Change-o Room the other day. Remember?" I wanted to wave my hand in front of him and say, "These aren't the droids you're looking for."

But he shrugged it off before I had to deny anything else. "Oh. Yeah. Right." Then he turned and walked away.

Diane cleared her throat and hurried out the front door.

Lurch and I stood looking after her, and as the funeral dirge played when she crossed the threshold, he said, "Thanks for visiting The Mansion. Please come again." I looked at him. He shrugged. "Mr. Stockton says it's my job to say that. He didn't say I have to mean it." It was more than I'd ever heard him say at one time, and I watched him return to his post at the door, my mouth hanging open.

In only a few minutes, I'd made my way to the tattoo parlor and unlocked the door that Harry had custom-made just for Dragons and Deities. It was a big arched door made of heavy weathered planks. Iron bars held the planks together, and the handle was a big iron ring.

He'd had it made the first time a female customer, a Bourbon Street stripper named Fiona the Fairy, had wanted a tattoo of a winged fairy emerging from the center of a lotus blossom on her booty, and there had been no way to give her privacy except by placing a screen in front of the table. Word had gotten around the resort somehow, and a lot of Looky Lous had shown up. A construction crew came the very next day, altered the doorway opening to the arch, and in only another couple of days, the door had arrived. Ever since, when a tattoo was requested on someone's private parts, I closed the door. It allowed for fewer distractions from the gallery.

The triplets, short, slim, and dressed alike—really?—showed up right on time at nine thirty. They loved the design I'd created of the three chimpanzees with their hands clasped respectively over their eyes, ears, and mouth. Their request had something to do with what their mother had said to them each and every night when she tucked them into bed as children.

One of them was done, and I was just getting ready to start the second tattoo when my cell phone rang.

"Excuse me." I moved away from the trio who were busy admiring the extremely hairy little sucker with his hands over his eyes and the mystical vines twining around him that I'd spent the last three hours inking on the client's upper arm.

"Hello?"

"Mel, it's Valentine."

"Hi, what's up?"

"I need a favor. A big favor."

"Sure," I said. "What?"

"We're short-handed in the kitchen. Aaron called in sick this morning. We're in the middle of lunch, and we've still got refreshments to put together for the memorial service this afternoon, and then comes dinner, and—"

I interrupted her. "So, I get it. You're up to your eyeballs. What do you need from me?"

"Benjy's at day camp. You know, the community center over by my place?"

"Yes. I know the one."

"Well, they're done after sack lunch at one, and I usually leave here for a bit to go pick him up and take him over to my sister's place for the rest of the day. But today, I'm just...I don't..."

"You want me to do it?" I looked over at the triplets who were still deep in discussion about the body art. "Let me see what I can do. I'll call you right back."

CHAPTER NINETEEN

———

The air was crisp and cool. The console on Valentine's little silver-grey Nissan four-door said it was only sixty-four degrees outside, but the humidity made it seem a little warmer. When the weather was calm, like it was on that Friday afternoon the day before Christmas Eve, it took about twenty or twenty-five minutes to drive from Mystic Isle to Valentine Cantrell's neighborhood in Estelle.

I'd sweet-talked the second of my trio of monkey tattoos into coming the next morning when his older-by-three-minutes brother was also scheduled for his appointment.

Valentine had handed me her car keys. "Oh, Mel, thank you so much."

"It's no problem," I'd said. And it really wasn't. The customers hadn't seemed to mind making a change, especially when I'd given them each a half-dozen drink coupons for the Presto-Change-o Room to smooth any ruffled feathers.

I'd driven the route before, having done this same favor for Valentine a couple of times in the past. Holidays and summer vacations were a definite challenge for single mothers, especially when something unexpected came up.

The community day camp center was in a strip mall on the main drag of the rural town where Valentine had chosen to raise her son. She'd called ahead and told them she was tied up and was sending someone over to pick up Benjy.

I pulled up and parked next to the curb in front of The Dollar Store and went inside the community center.

There were still about a dozen or so kids running around, watching cartoons, playing video games, and even a few reading actual books.

A heavyset woman with tired hair and even tireder eyes met me at the counter by the front door. Her name badge read *Agatha Thomas, Day Camp Counselor.* I'd never seen her there before.

"Yes?" She pushed hair off her forehead, but it just fell back down.

"I'm here to pick up Benjy Cantrell," I said. "His mother called ahead, and I'm on the authorized pickup list anyway." I fished my driver's license from my bag.

The counselor got a strange look on her face. It was something like a scared rabbit might look if cornered. When she took my license, her hand shook. She looked at it and handed it back to me. "You're the one Mrs. Cantrell called about?"

I smiled. "I am, all day long." It was something Granddaddy Joe used to say whenever anyone asked a similar question.

"I don't know what—" She turned away and yelled. "Thelma! Thelma, come quick!"

Another woman I didn't know, older but more alert and less hassled than Agatha seemed to be, was at the front desk in a flash. "What is it?"

Agatha swallowed hard. "This woman is here to pick up Benjy Cantrell."

The two women stared at each other a long beat. "But didn't you just say...?" Thelma spoke first. "Then who...?"

"Oh my God." Agatha said.

"How long?" Thelma said, the urgency in her voice apparent.

My stomach was starting to churn. Something was wrong.

Agatha rounded from behind the desk. "Only a few minutes."

"God, no!" Thelma threw up her hands and followed. They both leaned against the bar on the glass door, pushing it wide.

I turned and followed, hoping and praying that what appeared to have happened hadn't.

"There!" Agatha pointed across the parking lot and down the street. "That's the car she was in."

A green two-door compact headed away from the day care center. It was too far away to say what kind of car it actually was.

"Someone took Benjy?" My voice had gone up at least one octave maybe more. "Was it his aunt?"

Agatha shook her head. "A white woman. I didn't ask her name. Since Mrs. Cantrell called, I thought—"

I didn't hear what else she had to say, I was already out the door, sprinting across the parking lot. Throwing open the car door, I hopped in, slamming it shut. I pushed the ignition then screeched out of the parking lot like my hair was on fire.

Gas pedal smashed to the floor, heart nearly choking me, I steered like a maniac as I raced after the green car.

If it had been a movie, I would have picked up my cell and called the police or Valentine or both of them, but it wasn't a movie, and it was all I could do to keep the car on the road.

A light turned red in front of me, and I practically stood on the brake.

"Come on." I pounded the steering wheel. "Come on. Dammit."

After a few cars crossed the intersection in front of me, I looked both ways, took in a deep breath, and smashed down on the accelerator, shooting through the intersection against the light. "Hail Mary full of grace..." was all I managed to get out.

The green car turned left up ahead. I prayed there were no cops around to stop me for driving like a crazed woman on her way to a Macy's Super Saturday Sale. When I came to where the green car had turned left, I slowed down and made the turn carefully. It would have been cool to go careening around the corner, but I just didn't have the skill to do it on two wheels.

For a minute it looked like I might have lost them, but as I passed by General Jackson City Park, I saw the green compact parked under a big old willow tree in the shade.

Walking away were a small boy and a woman.

Benjy Cantrell.

And Diane Conner.

That bitch.

This wasn't good. *Duh.* Of course it wasn't good, but the fact that it was Diane Conner who'd taken him somehow made it even worse than I'd originally thought. What should I do? I had no earthly idea.

Staying at the edge of the parking area but close enough not to lose sight of Benjy and Diane, I dialed Quincy.

"Boudreaux."

"Quincy." It was a whisper—not sure why. I was alone in the car, but it seemed appropriate.

It obviously threw him off. "Is that you, Mel?" He laughed. "You trying to seduce me or something?"

"Shut up, Quincy, and listen. I'm at General Jackson City Park. Diane Conner took Valentine's son, Benjy. I've got my eye on them right now."

"Huh?"

"Really? I have to say all that again?"

Then the cop in him took over. "She took him? What does that mean?"

"Valentine sent me to pick Benjy up and take him to her sister's. When I got there, Diane had already come, taken him, and left."

"And Valentine hadn't sent her?"

"Of course not. Why would she send that nasty ol' thing? She's the last person Val would want around Benjy. I'm telling you that woman kidnapped him."

"General Jackson City Park. Is she armed?"

"How the heck should I know?"

"I'm too far away to help quickly, but I'll find someone close and send them right over." He stopped for a minute before adding, "Think you can keep an eye on them without landing right in the middle of it?"

Squinting against the sun's glare on the windshield, I could still see the two in the play area of the park.

Diane had plopped down on a bench, while Benjy headed for the swings. "Sure. No problem. I'll stay out of it. Just get someone over here, please, Quincy. As fast as possible. I'm scared."

After disconnecting the call, I debated whether or not to call Valentine. It was a decision I didn't have to make. My cell phone went off. Valentine's face appeared on the screen. The day camp must have already called her.

Before I could say a word, her panicked voice was in my ear. "Oh, Lord Jesus, Melanie. What's happening?"

I told her what I knew and reassured her that police were on the way.

"Why?" Her voice cracked. "Why would the Conner woman take my son?"

"I don't know why she took him, but I don't think she's going to hurt him, Val."

"That's my prayer," was all she said.

Across the grassy stretch between me and the boy, I saw Benjy slide out of the swing and run straight back toward where I'd parked. Diane jumped to her feet and yelled something, but I couldn't hear what was being said. Benjy kept coming, waving now.

The car. He recognized his mother's car.

Diane caught him and grabbed him by the arm, yanking him back toward her. The boy struggled but was too small to break loose, and she began pulling him across the park, away from the parking lot, away from me.

No police, no deputies, not yet. Where were they?

"Sorry, Quincy." I got out of the car, broke into a jog, and followed them, stopping at intervals, using clusters of trees for cover. She didn't move any faster, so it didn't look like she knew I was following them. But I needed help.

Valentine's voice was in my head. "Aaron called in sick this morning."

That meant he was at home. And from what I remembered, his place wasn't far from here. I scrolled through my phone and found his number that I'd put in yesterday when he offered to help clear Valentine.

He answered on the second ringtone. "This is Aaron."

"It's Mel."

"Oh." There was surprise in his voice. "What's up?"

I told him as quickly as I could.

Before I could even finish, he said, "On my way. Keep them in sight. I'll text and let you know when I'm there."

CHAPTER TWENTY

———

Diane picked up the boy and moved deeper into the park where there were fewer people. Benjy looked tense but didn't seem to be struggling against her or arguing.

I followed along.

Diane didn't turn around, didn't look behind her. Even if she had, I didn't think she could see me.

My cell phone vibrated in my hand. Aaron.

I'm here. How do I get to you?

I nearly wept.

I texted back with details. In less than a couple of minutes, he was at my side, his face flushed and anxious.

He sized up the situation in less than a minute and whispered, "Okay, here's what we do."

Our heads together, he laid out a plan of attack.

When he finished, I looked up at him. "I don't know if I can do this," I said. "But I'll do my best."

Quincy's question came back to me. "Is she armed?"

Armed? Scared. I was scared—for Benjy. For Aaron. And for me. But it didn't matter. I had to go through with it, and there was a good possibility we might all get through this without anyone getting hurt. Aaron's plan was pretty smart.

Aaron laid his hand on my shoulder and squeezed reassuringly. "You'll be great," he said, handing me his cell phone. "Don't worry."

I nodded. He turned, hunched down, and made his way around to my left, using trees and bushes for cover.

In the clearing in front of me, Diane had Benjy up in her lap. She was talking to him, her face serious. Benjy listened, shaking his head every now and then, nodding as well.

After waiting long enough for Aaron to get in place and set up, I looked down at the screen on his phone. He'd opened his music app. In the other hand, I opened mine, pulling up the song we'd chosen on both phones. Volume up as high as it would go. A phone in each hand.

Move out of the cover of the trees.

Take a deep breath. Control the nerves that churned in my stomach, quickened my heart rate, and made me take rapid, shallow breaths.

Now.

A phone in each hand, I pressed *Play*.

Miley Cyrus's "Wrecking Ball" blared from each phone. People a block away could probably hear it.

And I began to run, gathering speed until I was running full out straight at the bench where Diane sat with Benjy.

Diane's head jerked up in my direction.

Right on cue, Aaron stormed out of the bushes behind her and vaulted the back of the park bench.

Diane jumped up, her grip on Benjy still firm.

Diane's startled yell rose above the sound of the blaring music.

Aaron skidded back around, wrapping one arm around Benjy while he shoved Diane away with his forearm. She stumbled back, letting go of the boy, landing on her butt in the grass, but was back on her feet when I ran up.

Before she could come at either of us, I grabbed hold of Benjy's hand. "Come with me, Benjy."

He knew me, had seen me with his mother, and I'd picked him up from school and day care before. So, thank God, he never questioned me or hesitated, running with me across the yellowed winter grass until we stopped about twenty or so yards away.

Far enough Diane couldn't get to us.

But I didn't need to worry about her coming after us. Aaron had her prone on the grass face down, a hand on her neck, a knee on the small of her back. All the fight seemed to have gone out of her.

Her sobs carried on the wind, but Aaron didn't move or even look up. He was totally focused on her.

I pulled Benjy up against me and wrapped my arms around him.

"I want my mom." His small voice shook. "Where's my mom?"

From the direction of the parking lot, two sheriff's deputies ran toward us, pulling their guns as they ran.

A voice rang out. "Stay where you are."

They reached Diane and Aaron. One of the deputies, gun aimed, slowed down and approached them more slowly.

The other one stopped a ways back, keeping his weapon trained in their direction.

Another deputy came from the bushes behind me. He took hold of my arm and pulled me around to face him.

"What's your name?" he demanded.

"Hamilton," I said. "Melanie Hamilton. This is Benjy Cantrell. That woman over there, she—"

"I know, Miss Hamilton. Chief Deputy Boudreaux sent us. I just needed to make sure who you are." He knelt in front of Benjy who was now clinging to my leg, his frightened gaze riveted on the deputy. "Are you okay, son?"

Benjy gulped in air and nodded. My heart broke for him. He must have been scared half out of his wits.

The deputy looked up at me. "Why don't the two of you relocate to the parking lot, Miss Hamilton? We've got things covered here."

After looking, it was obvious the deputies did have things covered. Aaron was on his feet, hands waving around as he spoke beyond my hearing to the deputies.

Diane was now seated on the park bench, her head lowered, her hands covering her face.

I led Benjy back to the parking lot where Quincy was just pulling in.

One of the resort's gaily painted SUVs followed close behind his sheriff's unit. The SUV stopped, the passenger door flew open, and Valentine jumped out, her feet barely making contact with the ground before she ran to us.

The driver's side door opened, and Jack stepped out.

At the sight of him, all the courage from the adrenaline surge flagged, and the need to feel his arms around me bubbled up in barely contained tears.

Benjy jerked away as Valentine stopped running and knelt, her arms opening wide to pull him in.

The tears she held back were there in her voice. "What were you thinking, child? Going off with someone like that."

Benjy sobbed, his voice catching and breaking. "Sorry, Mom. She said you sent her. When I saw the car, I knew she wasn't taking me to you like she said. I was scared, Mom. I didn't know what..." He broke down, wailing now, shivering with reaction.

Hugging him to her, Valentine rose to her feet, her son against her chest. Her gaze fell on me. The crinkle of her eyes and the nod of her head expressed more gratitude than spoken words would have.

She turned and carried him back toward her car as Jack rushed up and threw his arms around me, his gaze roaming my face. "Thank God you're safe," he said. "When we got the call, I couldn't think about anything else but your safety."

I snuggled even closer to him, wrapping my arms around his back, burying my face against him. Breathing in the clean and manly scent I'd labeled Eau de Cap'n Jack, I relaxed. Safe. Benjy was safe. I was safe.

I twisted my head and saw Aaron walking toward us.

And Aaron was safe.

We were asked to make brief statements right there at the scene.

Agatha from the day camp showed up and identified Diane as the woman who'd come in and taken Benjy away.

Diane had been taken to Quincy's vehicle and placed in the back seat with the door remaining open. She yelled out every so often, demanding to be uncuffed and let go. She worked herself up into a near frenzy, hollering, "That slut doesn't deserve to have a beautiful child like that."

Quincy turned away from his conversation with Agatha. "Knock that stuff off, you hear?"

But Diane was on a roll. "Can't you all see I was doing him a favor taking him away from her? Why, she's a monster.

Bewitched Slim, led him down the Devil's road to an eternity of hellfire and brimstone. Good thing he died. If he hadn't died, he'd have been damned for sure."

While I didn't check to be certain, I felt pretty sure every head within the sound of her voice must have turned. Mine sure did. I stared at her. Beside me, Jack stared at her.

"What's that you're saying?" Quincy asked.

Diane looked around and seemed to realize she might have gone further than she intended. In a quieter, more subdued voice, she said, "Well, it's true. All of it."

"No wonder Slim sought out Valentine's calm spirit for advice," I said. "That woman's flat-out nuts." And I had to wonder if she'd go so far as kidnapping a child, wouldn't she also be capable of killing her husband.

CHAPTER TWENTY-ONE

————

I'd given Valentine her car keys back, and after making a call to the resort to be certain the food for the memorial service was taken care of, she and Benjy left for home.

Jack drove me back to The Mansion in the SUV.

We were still both pretty shook up.

"Did you hear what that Conner woman said about Slim getting killed?" he asked. "I mean, really? Who says that about their own husband?"

I didn't have an answer to the question but had one of my own. "Do you think she's crazy enough to have run that poor man down?"

He kept his eyes on the road and shrugged. "Don't know."

I sighed. "Me neither. But it'd be good for Valentine if she had, and even better if she'd admit it."

The sun through the windows was warm and comforting, making me a little drowsy. We drove the rest of the way to The Mansion in comfortable silence, arriving a little before three thirty. Jack dropped me off in front of his place then drove around to the fleet garage to return the SUV he'd signed out.

I had just enough time to take a five-minute shower, put my hair up in a messy little top knot, slather on some eye shadow and lipstick, and slip into the little black shift I kept at Jack's place in case we wanted to go out to dinner after work.

There were already quite a few chairs taken in the garden for the memorial service when I arrived exactly at four p.m. Jack was already there. I took the empty chair beside him and looked around. The white fold-up chairs were what the staff normally used to set up for weddings. But this wasn't a happy occasion. At least Harry had the good Southern taste to take down all the spooky Christmas decorations. That would have made it all pretty weird.

Many of the resort's employees were there: Stella, Cat, Lucy from the front desk, others—some I knew, some I didn't.

A jazz trio who worked the main salon a couple of nights a week had set up off to one side. They wound down from "Swing Low Sweet Chariot" and began "In The Garden," which seemed to be a cue for Harry who got up from his seat in the front row beside Fabrizio and mounted the two steps to where a podium stood on a raised deck.

Under one arm, he carried a Bible. Our fearless leader was dressed in the Harry Villars version of somber, wearing a pale blue suit over a dove-grey shirt, grey and blue striped bow tie, and leather mocs so close to the color of the suit they might have been dyed to match. Once he was behind the podium, he removed his signature Panama hat, today, white straw with a blue hatband, laid it on the seat of the chair beside him, and opened the Bible.

He removed a sheet of paper that had been marking the page, put on his glasses, and began to read Psalms 23 in a quiet, respectful voice, the lilt of his Louisiana accent lending a certain sweetness to the recitation.

Once he'd finished with the text, he opened the sheet of paper. "All of us here at The Mansion at Mystic Isle called our friend Phil Conner, Slim. It was a loving endearment to the man who readily acknowledged his love of good food, good liquor, and good times kept him rounder than some of us. More to love, I guess, like my own dear mother used to say. Slim always had a friendly smile and a good joke ready for anyone he encountered. He was a generous man, generous with his time and good spirits, and when he died, he been on a mission to make children happy. We're going to miss Slim. Yes, we are. And while I'm not a chaplain, I'm hoping those of you who pray will join me in the Lord's Prayer."

He bowed his head and began. "Our Father..."

I bowed my own head and began to say the familiar, comforting words. Beside me, Jack's voice joined my own, and the voices of sixty or so others commended Slim's spirit skyward.

When we were done, the jazz trio began to play "Amazing Grace," and Marvin, in a tiny tux fancy and well-tailored enough that it could have come straight off Rodeo Drive, went to the podium, pulled the chair over, and climbed up on top of it, smashing the crown of Harry's Panama hat in the process. He leaned in to the microphone and began to sing.

His voice was haunting and emotional. Even if the man was only three and half or four feet tall, his angelic voice gave him stature—well, that and the chair he stood on.

I was willing to bet by the time he finished there wasn't a dry eye in the house. It did kind of spoil the moment when he swung his arms and hopped down off the chair, his feet hitting the deck with a thump. But it looked like I might have been the only one who noticed because he was immediately surrounded by several fawning women from clerical and housekeeping, and of course Stella, who all gushed and *oohed* and *aahed* over his heartbreaking rendition of the old song.

Harry picked up the flattened hat off the chair, put his fist into the crown, and tried to push it back into shape. Still working on it, he stepped around Marvin and his fan club and bent to the mic again. "If you'd like to join us in the Presto-Change-o Room, there is a gorgeous buffet and open bar in honor of our friend."

With the sun lowering in the sky and a chill settling over the garden, we all made our way through the garden, across the pool deck, and into the French doors of the Presto-Change-o Room.

Warm air and the tantalizing aromas of the hot food from the buffet met us as we all filed inside and took over the venue.

The doors leading from the lobby into the Presto-Change-o Room had been closed and a *Private Party* sign set in front. As full as the hotel was with holiday guests, it was a tribute to Harry's and Jack's thoughtfulness and genuine concern that they were both willing to forego revenue the venue generated, especially on December 23, to pay homage to a friend and employee.

Jack and I had opted to wait until the lines at the buffet let up before checking it out. Cat and Stella came up to our table.

"Want some company?" Cat asked.

Jack got up and pulled out a couple of the chairs for them. "Of course," he said.

I had my eye on Cat's plate. She'd piled it high with Cajun wings, Andouille pigs in a blanket, some big old gorgeous pink shrimp, sweet potato fries, and chopped salad. My stomach grumbled, and all three of them looked at it. "I haven't eaten since breakfast." I shrugged.

"Well, you two go on," Cat said. "We won't let anyone take your places."

Jack sent me to the buffet while he headed for the bar. I loaded up a plate with enough food for us both and headed back to the table. He was right behind me with two iconic bottles of Ghost in the Machine brew from Parish Brewing.

I set the plate on the table between our two chairs and had almost put my butt back into the seat when I looked up and saw Odeo Fournet hovering nearby. I wouldn't have known him except for his bald head and neatly trimmed beard. I'd never seen the man wear anything except overalls, a work shirt, and boots. But today Odeo was dressed up like Sunday go to meetin' in a pair of khakis, a pale yellow sport shirt with embroidered columns on the front, and what could have been described as nurses' shoes only they were black.

Shifting from one foot to the other, looking around the room, he had a plate of food in one hand and a can of Coke in the other.

I waved at him, gesturing toward the empty chair at our table. He started over but stopped when he saw Jack. Odeo had always been a little nervous in Jack's presence, even if Jack had never really given him any cause. "Jack?" I said softly as he sat beside me. "Let Odeo know he's welcome to come and sit with us."

Jack looked up. "Oh, sure," he said, got back to his feet, crossed the space between our table and Odeo, took Odeo's plate from his hand, and led him back to us. Odeo shuffled his feet, hesitating to sit down until Jack said, "I'm so glad to see you, Odeo. It'll be nice to chew the fat with you." I smiled. It wasn't something Jack would have said a few months ago, but N'awlins was rubbing off on him.

That did the trick. Odeo sat down in the empty chair beside Stella and grinned. "I'm happy to see you too, Mr. Stockton. I been wantin' to talk to you 'bout that thing with Slim. You know? How he was sellin' that hooch out o' my shed?"

Jack looked up, chewing on a chicken wing. He swallowed and swiped at his mouth with a napkin. "Yes, Odeo? What's on your mind?"

"I was thinkin' 'bout this really old pirate I saw with Slim one night."

"Pirate?" Jack, Cat, Stella, and I said in unison.

Odeo nodded, serious as a guy at a tax audit. "A pirate in a Mardi Gras shirt." He raised one hand, three fingers together, like he was a Boy Scout. "I swear. They was walking together, and for all I know they might have been doin' some business. You know, like maybe having to do with all them spirits Slim had been haulin' out to my boathouse? Thing I remember about that old pirate was his shirt. It was different, you see. I never saw a shirt like that one afore. It was purple and green and gold, just like Mardi Gras, and the front of it said *Tip the Bartender*, and the back of it said *Chauncey's Roadhouse*."

Jack looked at me, one eyebrow arched.

"Chauncey's Roadhouse is just up the road," I said in explanation. "They pride themselves on 'Mardi Gras 24/7/365.' It's a biker bar. Everyone except the tourists know it's too sleazy to hang out in, and the liquor runs three times higher than it should."

Jack nodded, and we all turned back to Odeo to see what he had to add to his tale.

"If'n something was to go bad in the kind of deal they was makin', a man who'd buy bootleg liquor might not have any problems killin' off someone who'd done something he didn't like much." He spread his hands to let us know he'd pretty much finished laying out his theory. "What do y'all think 'bout that?"

"Hmm." That was Cat.

"Yeah." That was Jack. "You just might be onto something. But what makes you think he was a pirate?

"The patch. He had a pirate's patch on his eye. And a sword too."

"Odeo, that's so smart." That was me, and I was both giddy with the possibility of what he was saying and impatient that he hadn't said anything about this before. "It would have been good to know this before they hauled poor Valentine off to jail for the night."

Stella laid her hand on Odeo's arm in a calming gesture. She looked at me, her voice controlled. "Well, he's telling us now, Mel. Isn't that a good thing?"

Odeo's brows were knit together, his expression hurt.

I'd momentarily forgotten how sensitive and vulnerable The Mansion's grounds keeper was. I took a deep breath. "It is good, Odeo."

Odeo smiled, tied a napkin around his neck, and dug into his plate.

Jack, Cat, and I put our heads together while Stella chatted with Odeo about the upcoming takedown and storage of the holiday decorations and subsequent redecoration with the hearts and flowers for Valentine's Day.

We kept our voices low.

"We need to go to Chauncey's and find out who this guy is. What if he's the one who ran down Slim with the company van?" I said.

From across the room, Desi Lopez de Monterra came strutting in dressed in a three-piece magenta suit and matching tie. The suit fabric was splattered with jolly snowmen, sparkling snow crystals, and silver Christmas trees. The purple patent Cuban-heeled shoes with the hot pink block heels added a couple of inches to his diminutive height. The matching purple pocket square and zoot fedora were the perfect finishing touches to his zesty holiday costume.

He pranced by our table on his way to the stage.

"Mel." He stopped to lift my hand to his lips, raise his hot dark gaze to mine while he bowed low over one extended leg like a medieval courtier. "Man, you look slick tonight, mamacita."

Beside me, Jack bristled and put his arm across my shoulder. *Really, Jack? Men!*

"Why thank you, Desi."

He was such a player, a real ladies' man. And underneath all that swagger was a good soul who loved and cared for his mother and volunteered at the church every chance he got. Harry always kept Desi in mind when he needed a lone musician or even someone to sit in for another pianist.

Desi looked around the room that was full of those who'd attended Slim's wake. "Looks like you cats gave old Slim a real fine send-off," he said to Jack. "Only thing better would have been a second line parade."

Cat nodded.

Stella's smile was small and sad. "You got that right, Desi. Slim would've been knocked out with a second line parade." She and Desi high-fived across the table. "But this was real groovy. Especially what Marvin did. He just rocked it. Never knew I could be so attracted to such a small dude."

Desi grinned and wiggled his eyebrows. "Woman, you got no idea what a short man can do. Just because a dude's got short legs doesn't mean he short everywhere." He reached into his vest pocket with two fingers, slid out a big gold pocket watch, and flipped it open. "Well, guys and dolls, gotta run. My true love awaits."

"Your true love?" Stella actually sounded a little jealous.

"Yeah, my sweet baby with the ragtime rhythm." He jerked his head toward the stage.

A sudden thought occurred to me. "Could you wait just a couple seconds, Desi? There's something I'd like to ask you."

"Sure, doll. I always got time for a hot chick."

Yes, he was always a little over the top, but for some reason it never offended, probably because I never took him seriously. He was a lot like the outrageous skirt-chasing hound from *The Mask*. I half expected him to howl any minute.

Desi pulled an empty chair over from a nearby table, turned it around, and straddled it. "Lay it on me."

"Do you ever work at Chauncey's Roadhouse?"

He let his chin drop against his chest then looked up with a rueful expression. "Mmm. Not if I can help it, lovely. They ain't exactly what you'd call generous over there, and whenever I play there, I make sure I'm wearing body armor. But if they make an offer, and I don't have another gig, I figure why not. Low bread's better than no bread. Right?"

Jack saw where I was going. "Ever see"—he glanced at Odeo—"a pirate there?"

Desi looked at Jack and grinned. "Oh, sure, all the time" He did a double take when no one laughed. "You serious, cat?"

Jack nodded. "As a brain tumor."

Desi pulled off the fedora and ran his fingers through his hair to bring his poufy pompadour hairstyle back to life. "Pirate, eh?"

Odeo spoke up. "He has a pretty purple shirt from Chauncey's Roadhouse and a patch like a real pirate. And a pirate's sword too."

"Sword?"

"Oh, yeah. He was waiving it around in front of him when he walked."

Desi's dark eyes shifted to the side as he considered what Odeo said. "Oh. Yeah, man. You're talking about old Chauncey himself. But I'm pretty sure he had a cane, not a sword. Chauncey uses a cane. But Pirate?" He raised his hand to Odeo, and they executed an odd high-five—Desi's small, delicate, long-fingered musician's hand slapped against Odeo's huge, calloused gardener's hand. "Good one, man."

"So the guy with the patch is the owner?" I asked. "Chauncey?"

Desi nodded, reaching to snag one of the miniature pigs in a blanket hors d'oeuvres off Odeo's plate and pop it into his mouth. He chewed and swallowed. "Yeah, poor old Chauncey. Dude's about as old as the Mississippi and twice as crooked."

"Crooked?" Jack asked.

"I've heard stories about old Chauncey that'd keep you awake at night, but I never witnessed it firsthand. And I'm glad for that."

"So he's mean?" I asked.

"That's what I hear," Desi said, his eyes shifting toward the stage. "I better—"

Time to get down to it. "We think Chauncey had some backdoor deal going on with Slim Conner. It looks like Slim was stealing liquor from the resort and selling it out of the boathouse."

Desi shrugged. "For true? That surprises me. Slim seemed like a straight-up guy. But it ain't no big surprise about Chauncey. They say that cat's downright wicked."

CHAPTER TWENTY-TWO

———

Desi had gone to the stage and was pounding out a Dixieland version of "Jingle Bell Rock" on his ivory-keyed sweetheart, Zelda.

Employees of the resort and friends and associates of Slim Conner clustered here and there, eating, drinking, enjoying Desi's excellent music, and spinning tales about our recently departed friend.

After he'd finished eating, Odeo stood awkwardly. "I jes' want to thank all of you for letting me share this most solemn occasion with you." The way his brows knit together and his eyes shifted, I had the impression it was something he'd practiced saying and was working hard to get just right. "I'll be taking my leave now." He raised his chin and gazed up at the ceiling. "You wasn't one of my most favorite folks, but rest in peace anyway, Slim."

We all watched him leave. He carried himself with a lightness of motion and agility that was unusual for a man his size—almost graceful.

"What do you think about him?" Jack's face was marked with concern, consideration, and maybe even suspicion.

"About Odeo?" I asked. "What do you mean?"

"You think maybe he's laying a false trail? Trying to lead everyone away from the scuffle he's already admitted to having with Slim?"

I thought about it. "No," I said slowly. "No way."

Not Odeo. As Grandmama Ida would say, "That man doesn't have an ounce of guile in his whole body." I figured that was certainly true about sweet, almost childlike Odeo Fournet. At least I hoped it was.

But what Desi had told us about Chauncey, the bar owner, was still on my mind, and I guessed it must have shown on my face. "Hmm," I muttered.

Jack laid his forearms on the table and leaned in over them, his eyes narrowed. "You're not thinking what I think you're thinking. Are you?"

Uh-oh. Caught in the act. I shrugged. "That depends on what you think I'm thinking."

He sat back. "You're hatching a plan to check out this Chauncey guy."

"Maybe."

"I'm not going to let you do it."

"You're what? Not going to let me do it?" I huffed. "Don't know how you boys talk to women up in Yankee country, but down here, them's fightin' words."

"Let me rephrase that." Holding up his hands, he was the very definition of contrition. "I'm hoping you aren't planning to put yourself at risk by traipsing off to some biker bar and confronting a man who's at best been described as a pirate." He closed his mouth and waited for my response. None came, so he added, "How's that? Any better?"

I patted his hand. "Much. Thank you. But I can tell I may have to take you to raise, city boy."

He frowned. "Take me to what?"

"It's what Grandmama Ida always remarks when a man says some bonehead thing. She'll say that he needs to be taken to raise. You know, taught some decent manners."

Jack smiled. "I see. Well, my mom did teach me excellent manners, just sometimes I forget myself and say some bonehead thing, like when I'm worried a person I care a great deal about might be thinking of doing something I consider foolish."

"Well," I said. "If that person has a dear friend who's in danger of being charged with murder, and if a young child's life also rests on whether or not Papa Noël's gift bag is recovered, traipsing off to some biker bar seems like the least she can do."

He shoved back his chair, stood, and took a couple of steps.

"Where are you going?" I asked.

"To get my coat and car keys," he replied. "I'll be right back. If I can't talk you out of it, the least I can do is go with you. Besides, I haven't yet had the pleasure of experiencing a real Loosiana"—he pronounced it the way we did—"biker bar." He turned away and took another couple of steps but stopped again and said, "Think I need to wear my moto jacket?"

I shook my head. "No. I've seen that one. It's Saint Laurent. I think you'd be better off without it."

Chauncey's Roadhouse was only a few miles away from the resort. I'd been by it a few times on my way to Gretna, but I'd never had the nerve to stop and go in.

As we drove there I admitted, "Jack, I'm excited about this lead."

"Why's that?" He didn't look away from the dark country road. I didn't imagine he'd driven many roads like this one in his life, being a city boy and all. At night roads this dark could be fairly nerve wracking. Nothing much was visible beyond the reach of the headlights, and in the bayou it was possible anything could jump out in front—like a swamp rat the size of a golden retriever, or a gator, or maybe even a rougarou.

"I was running out of suspects and didn't want to nail down anything on those who are our friends and couldn't nail down anything on the ones who aren't. I'm fairly hoping this Chauncey guy turns out to be the one."

"Guess we'll see."

We had to pull around and park at the side of the building because the entire front parking area was taken up by Harleys, all lined up like little tin soldiers. There must have been a hundred of them.

Jack sat behind the steering wheel, looking at the place and running his hands back and forth around the rim.

"Something bothering you?" I asked.

He shook his head.

"Yes," I pressed. "Something is bothering you. Out with it."

"I think this might sound silly. Do you promise not to laugh?"

"Of course." I was dying to know what he was about to say.

"I'm kind of a movie freak."

"Yes, Jack, I know."

It was true. Jack Stockton was a walking Wikipedia when it came to movies. He could summarize the plot, name the cast and crew, hum the soundtrack, and even quote lines from just about any movie imaginable. But what did that have to do with Chauncey's?

"I can't tell you how many movies I've seen where people, people like us, normal people, walk into one of these places and get the living daylights beaten out of them by a bunch of good old boys with long hair, bushy beards, arms as big around as phone poles, and tattoos everywhere." He stopped rubbing the steering wheel, took his hands away from it, and opened his car door. "It's not that I'm scared or anything. I'm just trying to psych myself up for it."

It took every ounce of self-control I could muster up not to laugh. After all, I'd promised I wouldn't. I opened the passenger's side door and got out. "Jack, like you said, movies. You've seen *movies*. That's not the way these places are in real life. Don't worry about it."

He nodded like he'd accepted my explanation, but his mouth was set in a hard line, and as we went around the building, it seemed to me there was more than a little of that John Wayne trademark swagger in his walk.

On the outside Chauncey's looked like an old-fashioned general store with a weathered wooden porch that had seen so much traffic the boards were no longer flush to each other. The front entrance was made up of barn-style wooden doors that were just as weathered as the planks on the porch. The door handles were real, and I hoped unloaded, six-shooters. The sign on the door read *Smoke 'em if you got 'em.*

"Look at that," I said. "Quaint."

"Yeah," Jack said dryly. "Charming."

We each took hold of a pistol handle and pulled, opening the doors to what could only be described as complete and utter pandemonium. It was exactly as Jack had thought, just like in the movies. Zydeco music so loud I could feel its rhythms in my chest. Laughter. Shouting. The clank of silverware, dishes, and glasses. The smells of burgers and fried fast food. Smoke thick as a fog bank in the air.

I'd have to take a shower when this was all over.

Jack coughed. "Like I said"—he leaned close and spoke right beside my ear—"just charming."

The cement floor had been painted purple. The walls were sort of gold. The upholstery on the booths was green. Desi had said they prided themselves on being Mardi Gras 24/7/365. Here and there red and silver aluminum garlands were draped overhead. The support pillars were wound with strands of Christmas lights, the old kind with the big bright flame-shaped bulbs, like my grandparents used to string up when I was a kid.

We made our way through the place, weaving around dancers and waitresses wearing Daisy Dukes with tight red sweaters and Christmas tree-green knee socks in a nod to the season.

A couple of men who had to have been seven feet tall if they were an inch got up from their barstools and pushed past us. Both were heavily bearded with, I thought back to what Jack had said, "...arms as big around as phone poles and tattoos everywhere."

Jack squeezed my hand and sort of pulled me around behind him.

But instead of challenging us, they both nodded and smiled. "Merry Christmas," the first one said.

"Happy holidays," said the other.

"Back at ya," I said.

"Yeah, to you too," Jack said.

The two moved on, and we took their stools at the bar, each ordering a beer—drafts. The bartender, a tall, slim guy with the odd combination of long grey hair pulled back into a ponytail and a handlebar moustache so thick and black it almost looked as if it had been drawn on, set the glasses in front of us.

Jack shoved a twenty-dollar bill across the bar. "Keep the change." The bartender saluted as Jack went on. "Is the owner here?"

"Chauncey?" I added.

The bartender lifted his chin and pointed with the hand holding a bar rag. "Over there. Guy in the corner booth."

We both looked across the bar area to a darkened corner booth. There were two men in there, but it was so dark we couldn't make out anything about them.

We took our beers and made our way over there. Now that we were closer, we could see that one of the guys definitely looked, just as Odeo had said, like a pirate.

Jack reached for his wallet, making me wonder what he had up his sleeve.

When we stopped in front of Chauncey's table, Jack held out his hand. "Are you Chauncey?" he asked.

Turning his head, Chauncey, the man with the eye patch, nodded. "Da be fo sho, son. Whtcha bened?" His voice was gravelly, his Louisiana accent so thick even I wasn't quite sure of what he'd said. The nod of his head was enough to answer Jack's question. He must have been Chauncey, and he did look a little like an old pirate as Odeo had said.

The deep lines on his face were tracks of an interesting life. His salt and pepper but mostly salt hair was long and scraggly. The T-shirt he wore tonight was a gold one with *Chauncey's Roadhouse—where Mardi Gras lives all year long* scrolled across the front.

But he didn't accept Jack's offered hand.

"My name's Jack Stockton. I'm the manager over at The Mansion on Mystic Isle." Jack gave up trying to get the man to shake and held out a business card. Chauncey didn't reach for it. "We were wondering if perhaps you'd be interested in a joint promotion between Chauncey's Roadhouse and The Mansion."

Chauncey still wasn't looking at us. "Mmm." It was a growl, more like a grunt really.

The man in the booth beside Chauncey, who I'd hardly even looked at, reached out, took it, and stuck it in the pocket of Chauncey's T-shirt. "There ya go, Pops," he said.

Jack and I both turned toward the other occupant of the booth. He was young, only in his late teens or early twenties. He wasn't good-looking but wasn't bad-looking either, just a normal guy with a normal build, shaggy hair, and a face I probably wouldn't be able to remember tomorrow.

"Chauncey's my grandpops," he said. "We don't do— what'd you say?—joint promotions here. We got no need." He waved his hand around the room. "Plenty o' business just seems to kinda fall in our laps."

"Mmm." Chauncey grunted again. He still hadn't looked at us.

"Good boy," Chauncey grunted, one hand groping around the table until he found what appeared to be an old-fashioned monocle that was thick as a Coke bottle bottom. He held it up to his face, and finally for the first time he looked up at us.

"Der ya be." At least I thought that was what he said.

Jack and I both stared wordlessly.

"Oh," Jack said, turning away from Chauncey and back to the grandson. "I see. So your grandfather wouldn't be interested in anything like that?"

"Wut wrong wid you?" the old man said. "I blind not deaf."

"Sorry," Jack said. "It was just...your grandson...I..." Finally, he just gave up and shrugged. "Thanks for your time, Mr. Chauncey. I can see—" He stopped, realizing what he'd said and cringed. "I can *tell* you probably don't need to garner additional business, so we'll just say good evening to you and thank you for your time."

The place suddenly grew much quieter as the band stopped playing. The bartender stepped up to the microphone. "Ladies and gents, it's time for our Friday night karaoke contest."

The grandson stood. "Pops needs you to leave now. He has to go be the judge for the karaoke."

"Judge?" I asked.

"Tree nights I is," Chauncey said.

"Tree nights." I repeated.

The grandson walked around in front of us and laid his hand on Chauncey's arm. "Three nights," he clarified. "Fridays, Saturdays, and Sundays from six to ten are Chauncey's Roadhouse Karaoke Battle Nights. Pops is the judge, the only judge. He hasn't missed a night in what..."

"Fortu yar." Chauncey's lined face split into a huge grin. As close as we were, I could see he needed to spend some of the money a place like this probably brought in at a dentist's office.

"Forty-two years. That's right. Rain or shine. Hale and hearty or doing poorly. Pops is here to judge and award the prize, twenty steak dinners, to the winner."

I had to make sure what I was hearing. "Every Friday, Saturday…and…Sunday from five to ten, your granddaddy's here judging this contest?"

Chauncey slid over to the edge of the seat and placed his hand on his grandson's forearm.

"Never missed a night," the younger man said.

"Not even last Sunday night?"

"No damn way," Chauncey said.

I had no trouble understanding that.

"So nows I'm gwan judge. You g'on den," Chauncey's head was tilted in our general direction. "Git."

Jack and I went back out to the parking lot and got into the SUV. We sat looking at each other a beat before both bursting into laughter. When we stopped laughing, I said, "Well, I'm thinking Chauncey, who doesn't appear to be able to see his hand in front of his face, probably couldn't even find the van, much less manage to get it started and run over Slim not once but twice.

Jack hit the ignition, and the engine turned over. "That poor old guy'd be more likely to run it through a wall or into the river than be able to steer it straight enough to hit someone on purpose."

"But don't forget what Desi had to say about him. He said he'd heard how the old man is downright mean."

"Sure," Jack said, "And we know he was buying bootleg liquor from Slim who probably wasn't his only supplier."

I sighed. "Chauncey the pirate might not be one of the good guys, but I'm not thinking he managed to kill Slim and take the Christmas donations. With a place like this, I'm betting he's a rich old man, and what that bag held wouldn't be worth murder to him."

"Plus he seems to have an airtight alibi," Jack said. He put the car in reverse and backed out of the parking lot, heading back toward The Mansion. "Karaoke night, eh? We should come over some night and take a shot at it."

"You, Yankee boy, maybe you should come on over some night and take a shot at it. This southern girl can't sing a lick, and she knows her limitations."

"Yeah?" Jack reached across, took hold of my hand, and squeezed. "We'll see about that."

We rode the rest of the way in silence. I didn't know what Jack was thinking, but seeing that we'd just come up another blind alley, I wondered if we were ever going to exonerate Valentine and get the money needed for Nicole's treatment.

CHAPTER TWENTY-THREE

———

It was a little after six thirty when we walked back into the ornate oval lobby of the resort. I was glad to see Lurch in his usual somber black suit at his usual spot just inside the double doors. His only nod to the holiday season this evening being a headband sporting antlers, holly berries, and jingle bells. The antlers bobbed around when he moved his head.

Jack lifted a hand as we walked by him. "Lookin' good tonight, Lurch."

Lurch just groaned but did high-five Jack.

Over at the reception desk, a man's voice was on the rise.

Lucy stood in her designated spot behind the counter, arms crossed, trying to keep a smile pasted on her face.

The man in front of the counter, the man pounding his fist on the marble top, was none other than my current number-one suspect, the bookie, Zachary Jones.

"And why can't you tell me, Lucy? Fifty's not enough? Would a Ben Franklin do it for ya?" He reached for his back pocket.

Lucy shook her head and held her hands up, palms out. "Mr. Jones, please. I can't—"

Jack took four long strides, and he was there beside Zachary. "Something I can do to help you, Mr. Jones?"

The bookie turned, his eyes narrowed as if he was trying to remember. He pointed an index finger. "Stockton, right? You're the manager."

Jack offered his hand. "Is there a problem?"

Zachary shook with Jack. "I'm just trying to convince Lucy here to part with a little information I need."

Jack's smile looked so authentic, I was probably the only person in the room who knew it wasn't. "And what would that be?"

"She told me Diane Connor was no longer a guest here." Jack glanced at Lucy. "That's right."

"Well, I need to know where she went." Jones said. "She's not at home. I checked." He lifted his chin. It looked a little bit like a challenge.

So, now the bookie was stalking poor, screwed-up Diane? I thought about it, considering that maybe Cat and I were lucky to have made it out of his sports book safely. If I had it to do over, I probably wouldn't have taken the risk. If Zachary Jones killed Slim and was looking for Diane, he was dangerous.

And he certainly looked the part in a black long-rider coat and a black flat-brimmed undertaker's hat. He looked like an old-time gunslinger out to take care of business. I fully expected him to mumble, "I'm your huckleberry."

But instead he said, "If you know where she is, Stockton, I can make it worth your while to tell me."

I was still a good eight to ten feet away from them, but I could tell Jack was angry from where I stood. He cleared his throat, probably to keep the anger from it. "Mrs. Conner isn't here."

Zachary narrowed his eyes. If he'd had a moustache, he'd have been stroking it. "Hmm. Not here. Not at home. You think she left the area?"

"No." Jack shook his head, his tone ironic. "Pretty sure she hasn't left the area."

The bookie stared at Jack a few beats then turned his glare on Lucy.

She shrugged and tried to smile but was clearly upset.

"You people know her loser husband owed me a boatload of money, right?" His voice was tight.

Neither Jack nor Lucy answered him.

He went on. "So I'm looking for his wife. In my business, we expect someone to stand good for a man's debts. Even after he dies. If she knows what's good for her..." His voice trailed off.

I swallowed—hard.

Jack's jaw clamped shut, and his face went hard. I stared at him. I'd never seen that look on his face before or heard that steel in his voice. "You wouldn't be threatening a man's widow now. Would you, Mr. Jones?"

Zachary shrugged, but he didn't look away, and the serious expression on his face was more than enough of an answer.

"Really?" Jack said. "Doesn't sound like a good idea for a man who makes illegal book and is maybe even a homicide suspect to be tossing around hints that he might be going after a sick, grieving woman. What do you think? Sound like a good plan to you? A person might believe a man who'd threaten a woman wouldn't think anything about killing a man."

Jones stepped away suddenly and practically shrieked, "Homicide suspect?"

He looked around the room as if he expected a SWAT team to jump out from behind a pillar and arrest him. "What makes you think I'm a suspect in Conner's death?"

Jack's voice was calm and even, like he was explaining unexpected charges on a bill to an irate guest. "Death? You mean murder. Don't you? Well, let's see. You were here that night, captured for posterity on the digital video, with enough time in between your arrival and departure to have done the deed. And you've made it plain you had a serious problem with Slim. Why *wouldn't* you be considered a suspect?"

I looked back and forth between Jack and the bookie. The way Jones was dressed, I almost expected him to draw a six-shooter and fill my man full of lead. He brushed aside the coat and reached inside.

I drew in a sharp breath and said, "Wait!"

But Jack and Zachary Jones just kept staring at each other like cowboys at high noon.

"Wait for what?" Jack said, his eyes still fixed on Jones.

I felt a little foolish. This was Mystic Isle, not Dodge City, and it was the 21st century, not the 19th.

Everything slid back into perspective when Zachary relaxed and shoved the brim of his hat back a bit. "You people watch too much television. Why on earth would I want to kill someone who owed me fifty-two large? That doesn't make any sense—I'd be in exactly the crappy situation I'm in today. Out an enormous amount of money and nowhere to turn for payment. You must think I'm an idiot." He looked around the lobby and said loudly, "Does *anyone* here know where I can find Mrs. Conner?"

The few people in the lobby looked up in confusion.

I moved over beside Jack and cleared my throat, anxious to get rid of Zachary Jones and the tension he brought with him. "You might check with the sheriff's office," I said.

He looked at me, blinking. His voice seemed to have risen in pitch. "Why would I want to talk to someone at the sheriff's office?"

"Because," I said, "the sheriff will know how you can get in touch with Diane Conner. They took her into custody a few hours ago."

Zachary Jones went pale and opened his mouth to speak, but nothing came out. He turned abruptly toward the front door and walked quickly away, looking around and back over his shoulder as he went.

We watched him go.

Lurch saluted as he left. "Thank you for visiting The Mansion, sir. Have a Merry Christmas."

I wasn't sure, but I thought I saw Zachary Jones give Lurch the bird.

"Mr. Jones seem a little nervous when you brought up the sheriff?" Jack asked.

"Little bit," I said. "Yeah."

Seeing Jack go up against Zachary Jones without flinching. Exciting.

Realizing Jones wasn't the badass he represented himself to be. Enlightening.

Seeing the big bully speechless. Priceless.

Jack and I stopped at the employee locker room where I picked up my overnight bag, and then we walked across the grounds to Jack's little domicile.

After his shift, Quincy planned to cross the river and spend the night at our place with Cat. Awkward—for me anyway. I'd twice caught him in his tighty-whities, bum turned up, head stuck down, rummaging through the refrigerator in the middle of the night. It hadn't seemed to bother Quincy. The first time he'd just straightened up, waved a fried chicken leg at me, and gone back to Cat's bedroom, and the other time he'd poured a glass of milk and stood there in his briefs talking to me about how most people never got enough calcium and vitamin D in their diet. Then there was the time I'd left the house early and walked down to Café du Monde at the French Market for some warm breakfast beignets only to return to find Quincy strolling out of my shower, a towel wrapped around his head and nothing else.

"Oops," he'd said. "Cat's having a bubble bath in the other tub. Thought you wouldn't mind if I used your shower."

I'd been so traumatized I'd gone back outside and ate all the beignets myself. You just can't unsee something like that, and the handsome Cajun didn't seem to have a modest bone in his studly bod.

So when Cat told me she and her lover boy were having a slumber party at our place, I'd asked Jack if he was up for a sleepover at his place.

"You betcha I am," he'd said.

As we walked across the grounds under a clear night sky, I pointed at a bright star low on the horizon. "That one's Venus," I said.

"Yeah? How do you know?"

"Stella," I said. "She knows all the stars and planets, where they are, what they portend to us?"

"Nice," Jack said, swinging our clasped hands between us. He was quiet for a while then said, "That bookie is an interesting guy."

"Where do you think he got that outfit?" I asked. "That'd look real sexy on you. If you had one, we could do some role-playing, pretend you're the nameless gunslinger in town, and I'm the schoolmarm."

He brought my hand to his lips and kissed it, a wicked glint in his eye. "Let's hurry on over to my place and check out that scenario."

"But you don't have the outfit," I said.

"Outfit?" He pretended to snarl. "I don't need no stinking outfit."

CHAPTER TWENTY-FOUR

———

I sat straight up when my cell phone went off. I'd fallen asleep waiting for Jack to come back. He'd been called away when the alarm had gone off at Harry's house, *la petite maison*. Harry and Fabrizio were spending the night across the river in one of those fabulous hotels in the Quarter. They'd spent the day Christmas shopping and the evening attending a performance of *The Nutcracker* at the Saenger Theatre.

The phone rang with "Aquarius." It was Stella. My phone screen said it was after ten. "What the heck?"

I clicked on the call, and before I could even speak, the tone of Stella's voice alerted me that something was wrong. "Oh, thank the stars, Mel. I'm so glad I got hold of you. I'm so scared. Can you help me?"

It was one of those questions you weren't sure you should just say yes to, but I never seemed to learn and said, "Of course. What is it?"

"My client. Zachary Jones. He called me. Threatened me. Said he's coming here. When he got back to his place, the police were there, asking him questions about Slim Conner, and he's worried they'll find out about his whole book business and shut him down or worse, send him to prison. And he's fit to be tied, Mel. Says he knows it was me who narced him out. It wasn't, but how do I make him believe that? He's coming. Coming to get me. What should I do?"

So the police were sniffing around Zachary Jones, eh? Perfect. Except it wasn't good for Stella. I had heard the fear in her voice. Stella by Starlight, one of the most laid back persons I'd ever run across had screeched so loud I'd had to hold the phone away from my ear.

"I'm at Jack's, but I'll go to the main building. Lock your house. Get in your minivan and come here. Right away. I'll meet you in the employee lounge, but first I'll find someone to hang out with us, someone bigger and stronger than we are, so if Zachary shows up here, there won't be any trouble."

"Yes." She was breathless. "I'll be right over."

It wouldn't take long for her to drive back to The Mansion from her place in Lafitte.

My mind raced. Jack wasn't here. He'd been called away when the alarm had gone off at Harry's place. I tried to call him but just got voicemail. "It's me. There's trouble. Please hurry back." Before I clicked off, I added, "Hurry, Jack."

What was I going to do? Who could I get? Odeo knocked off work at six, and he lived all the way across the river in New Orleans with his sickly mother. Lurch's shift was over by now too.

But Aaron Bronson. Yes! His place in Estelle wasn't far from Valentine's, and definitely not too far from The Mansion. He could well have the breakfast shift in the morning, have to get up at three, and hate me for calling him this late. But if Zachary Jones, bookie and possible murderer, was coming all the way here to get even with Stella for something she hadn't even done…well, I was willing to risk making Aaron a little miffed at me just to get him over here to take care of things.

After a few rings, he answered. "Yeah?"

"Aaron, it's Mel Hamilton. I need help. Well, not me exactly. It's Stella. That crazy bookie guy is on his way to her house to hurt her."

"Huh?"

Every second counted, so I rushed through the story as quickly as I could, explaining everything about Jack, and Odeo, and the security guards, and Stella, and Zachary Jones—finishing up with, "I know it's a lot to ask, but how long would it take you to get here?"

"I am here," he said. "I worked late. Thought I'd take a few laps in the pool before heading home."

A huge weight lifted off me. "Oh, thank God. The indoor pool?"

"Well, yeah," he said. "It's December. Didn't want to freeze my butt off."

"Right. Stay there. I'm on my way."

I hung up, slipped my shoes back on, and left Jack a note. Crossing the grounds from Jack's cottage to the main building, I remembered what I'd been dreaming about when Stella's call woke me.

I was in a cemetery. At night. Cold. Granddaddy Joe kept showing me a shovel, and when I asked him what he wanted me to do with it, all he said was, "Whomp wid it." Whomp. Weird.

It only took me about five minutes or so at a slow trot to get to the main building. I was still out of breath. I was anxious, worried, and feeling more than a little guilty. Without knowing for sure, I was pretty confident the reason the NOPD had been around to the sports book was because I'd given Chief Deputy Boudreaux a heads up to check that guy out.

And now Stella might be in danger because of it.

I let myself in through the back patio doors and made my way around to the indoor pool.

It was surprising to find the main door unlocked. Harry always insisted the place be locked up after ten.

Aaron was still swimming, his long arms arcing over before slicing back through the water. His clothes, towel, a key to the pool door, and some other personal items lay poolside. I walked over by them and knelt down.

Aaron was doing a flip at the far side of the pool and headed back in my direction.

I reached over and picked up the big fluffy towel as he started back on what I was going to insist would be his last lap. I needed him dressed and ready for whatever was coming our way, if anything. I didn't know for sure Zachary Jones would go so far as to come here looking for Stella, but I wouldn't put it past him, and I had a really queasy feeling about this whole thing.

As I shook out the towel, a small object flew out and clanked against the pool tiles. "Oops." I picked it up and looked at it.

Dog tags on a chain. I remembered that Aaron had said he'd served in the military on a bomb squad. Curious, I took a quick look at the tags, frowning as I read the inscription.

But the tags didn't appear to be Aaron's.

I read silently, my lips moving: Tyrell R. Cantrell. Followed by a Social Security number. O Positive. Christian.

Tyrell Cantrell. I looked up from the tags just as Aaron closed in. His hand found the edge of the pool, and he climbed out, running one hand back through his hair, shaking the water from his face.

He looked down, smiling. "So, you ladies need a hero?" He laughed. "I'm your…"

His gaze fixed on the tags in my hand then moved quickly away. He held out his hand. "Towel?"

I handed it up to him, got my feet under me, and stood. "These aren't your dog tags." *Duh, Melanie.* But I was too confused to say anything else.

Aaron was scrubbing the towel over his wet head, down along his arms. He pulled it around the back of his neck and let it hang there.

"No," was all he said. "I lost mine a long time ago. Those? Hell, I won those in a poker game a while back."

"But why would you wear someone else's…" I let it hang there.

"Just wanted to have a set. You know how it is. You get used to something." His voice was as smooth as ever, but suddenly I wasn't buying the story.

"So you didn't know Tyrell Cantrell?"

He shrugged. "Tyrell Cantrell? The guy on the tags? No. To me, that's just a name on the tags I wear to remind me of my deployment."

No way on the face of God's green earth something like this could just be a coincidence. *He wears the dog tags of Valentine Cantrell's deceased husband and shows up here to work with her, rents an apartment only a few minutes from her house. Nope. Not a chance.* I opened my mouth to challenge his story but could swear I heard someone say, "Keep your trap shut." It had the ring of Granddaddy Joe's voice, but lately I tended to think I just imagined my inner voice sounded like him.

"Hmm," I said. "I get it. You don't have tags to wear, but for sentimental reasons, you just wear these."

He nodded, but he was watching me pretty close.

I smiled, or tried to, and shrugged. "Okay, well. Why don't you get dressed, and meet me in the lobby? Stella ought to be here any minute, and we can figure out what to do if that Zachary guy follows her here."

After a pause, he said, "Sure. Just give me a sec."

Something was wrong. So wrong, but I wasn't sure what it was. My stomach churning, my brain on overload, I smiled at him. At least I thought I did.

Aaron Bronson wore the dog tags of Valentine Cantrell's deceased husband, a man who died serving in the military over seven years ago.

And he won them in a poker game? No freakin' way.

I'd only taken a step or two away when Aaron said from behind me, "Sorry you had to see those, Mel. I really am."

I started to turn around, but he wrapped one arm around my neck from behind and pulled me up against him, pushing down against my head with his opposite hand. My airway was cut off. Struggling, I tried to remember how to get out of a choke hold from all the movies I'd seen—hands down, hips thrust back, stomp on the toe. It didn't work, even though he was barefoot. He grunted but tightened his grip on my neck, and as my vision darkened, I thought I heard him say, "Maybe you should have minded your own damn business."

Everything went black, and then—nothing.

CHAPTER TWENTY-FIVE

———

It was windy. The air blowing across me was cold. Sounds of the bayou—water slapping against the shore, night animals serenading each other. The odd smell of ancient swamp assaulted my nostrils. I was outside, lying on the cold, damp grass.

My throat hurt.

Another sound. What was it? Scraping. Something was scraping against the ground. In the few seconds as I regained consciousness, I grew more and more aware of my surroundings. Someone was here with me. Labored breathing underlay the scraping sound.

I remembered then.

Aaron. Aaron had attacked me, and now I was outdoors in the cold. And someone was with me. There was no doubt in my mind it was him.

Opening my eyes to a slit, I tried to see what was going on without alerting him I'd awakened.

Aaron was only a few feet away, and he was dressed now. Beyond, the full moon illuminated the gravestones. Well, crap. I was back in the cemetery—just like in my dream. And Aaron was working on one of the old graves. Digging. That was the sound I'd heard.

I tried to think, but my head was still fuzzy from the choke hold the creep had laid on me. *Lie still. Make a plan.*

Right. But what?

He stopped digging, buried the blade in the dirt, and leaned on the handle. He stood still a moment, and even though his face was in shadow, I could feel his eyes on me.

I didn't move.

After a minute, he said, "I know you're awake. The rhythm of your breathing's changed. Won't do you any good to play possum."

Good thing I never had aspired to be an actress.

I opened my eyes and looked right at him. "What's going on, Aaron? What are you doing?"

"Don't be coy," he said, standing up straight and yanking the shovel from the ground. "You know what I'm doing, and you know why."

He must have been hanging around a different kind of Louisiana woman. "I'm never coy, Aaron. And I don't know."

He hauled out another shovelful of moist Louisiana dirt and tossed it aside. "You saw the tags."

"Tyrell Cantrell's tags."

He kept digging, his words separated by the ragged breaths he drew as he dug. "I served under Sergeant First Class Cantrell in Afghanistan. We were EODs, Explosive Ordnance Disposal. He took one for the whole platoon. Died for us. For me. I swore I'd watch over his woman and son, keep them safe for him, whatever it took."

He almost seemed to have forgotten I was even there, speaking more to the night and the cold wind than to me. "After I came back, I found her. Five years I've been keeping my eye on her now. And things were going great until that lousy bartender started running around with her, ruining her reputation. I couldn't let it go on, you see."

Until that very moment, I hadn't put it all together. But there it was. In a stupid and misguided gesture to protect Valentine's honor, Aaron had killed Slim Conner.

Now he was digging in the cemetery, and I didn't figure he was just trying to build up his muscles.

My voice was gravelly. "But the Sheriff blamed it all on her. How's that taking care of her?"

He grunted with the effort of shoveling dirt from the grave. "That wasn't supposed to happen. I had it figured she was so far above reproach if I used her boots, no one would think anything about it. Besides, all the boots in the locker room were muddy. I didn't believe it when they zeroed in on hers."

I didn't know what to do, but getting up and running seemed like a pretty good idea. I was shaking and didn't know if it was from the cold or from fear—or both.

His shovel clanked against something hard. A coffin. They were always laid in pretty shallow here in the bayou, and he hadn't had to dig down very far. With the blade, he leveraged the shovel against the lid of the coffin, and suddenly, his plan was pretty darn clear. He was going to kill me and dump me in with the other corpse, whoever that poor soul was.

But I didn't plan on making it easy for him.

Rolling onto my side, I pushed off the ground, brought my feet up under me, and launched myself away—only to have the wind knocked completely out of me as I sprawled flat. He'd hit me in the back with the shovel.

Trying to suck air back into my deflated lungs, I sounded like an out-of-tune accordion, wheezing and squeaking. The pain was excruciating. He rolled me over with the toe of his boot. And I looked up into his shadowed face. "Let's not make this any harder than it has to be, Mel." He reached down and grabbed hold of the front of my jacket. "Whaddya say?"

He began to lift me, and if I didn't do something, I knew he'd kill me—probably do something violent and bloody with the shovel. The way he straddled me, his soft parts were open and vulnerable, I brought up one leg, but the position I was in didn't allow me to put much force behind it.

My targeting was spot on, but without being forceful, it didn't bring him down the way I'd hoped.

"Bitch. Why is it you women always aim there?"

My shoulder and butt were off the ground, and he stepped over me, starting to drag me back toward the rancid, dirt-covered coffin.

"Please." It was all I could think of to say. "Just…please."

"Too late. Should have thought about the consequences sooner. Don't you—"

Something big and fast and solid hit us. It was like being slammed into by a locomotive. Aaron and the driving force went one way, while I went the other, hitting the ground and rolling over a couple of times.

When my senses found me again, I could see Aaron and what looked like a bear wrestling together on the ground.

Aaron got the upper hand and forced my would-be rescuer to the ground. "Idiot. I'm trained in combative techniques. All you got is mass. You can't beat me."

It was Odeo who'd come flying across the graveyard faster than I'd ever thought a man his size could move. Odeo, who'd knocked the two of us apart and taken on the killer, and if I didn't do something fast, it would be Odeo who'd die here with me on this cold, dark December night.

Up onto my knees then crawling, I made my way closer, no idea what I was going to do to stop him. That was when the voice spoke to me—my inner voice, the one I could have sworn was my Granddaddy Joe sending me messages from the other side. "Whomp him wid it, Mellie gal. Whomp."

Ah-ha!

Stretching out my arm until my fingers curled around the handle, I dragged it closer, using it to help me to my feet.

Just a couple of feet ahead of me, Aaron had his forearm on Odeo's throat. Poor Odeo's eyes were enormous in the moonlight.

Hefting the shovel up and across my body so I could send it with as much force behind it as possible, I swung it with my full weight behind it.

My cell phone went off. "A Pirate's Life for Me." It was Jack.

Aaron's head jerked around, his expression murderous. He lifted one hand to block my swing, but it was too late.

The shovel came down across the side of his face, knocking him off Odeo, sending him flailing onto the cold, wet grass, where he lay still.

Odeo was gasping for air but had enough energy left to haul himself to his feet.

My phone was still signaling, and I answered it with, "Jack. Cemetery. Come now. Call the police. It was Aaron. All the time, it was him." I ran out of breath but still managed to choke, "We need you. I need you."

I dropped to my knees as Odeo dragged Aaron by the arm across the grass to the sunken coffin, the one with the lid pried off, the one Aaron had intended to bury me in.

Dumping Aaron on the ground beside the gaping hole, he bent and used both hands to roll the unconscious murderer into the waiting coffin to lie with the bones of one of Harry Villars' ancestors. At least until Jack arrived with the cavalry.

Odeo looked up at me. "You okay, Miss Melanie?"

I sighed and nodded. "Sort of," I said. "You?"

"Yes'm," he said, rubbing his throat. "Though I have been some better."

"Yeah. Me, too."

CHAPTER TWENTY-SIX

———

Time seemed to stand still as Odeo and I sat in the cold, damp cemetery with only the moonlight to see by.

Odeo hummed incessantly, his low bass tones reverberating into the night. His choice of songs? "Grandma Got Run Over by a Reindeer." Sounds of the bayou night served as his rhythm section, syncopating the tune.

Come on, really? His humming and especially his choice of songs irritated me, and I wanted to ask him to stop, but the big guy was probably in the same shape I was—mainly, exhausted and scared. So I just sat on a boulder while he paced in front of me. That silly song would probably be running through my head forever.

Jack and one of the resort's security guards came on the scene only a few minutes before my nemesis, Sergeant Mackelroy, and another deputy from the sheriff's office arrived and hauled Aaron out of the moldy coffin.

Jack hugged me closer than close, as if shielding me from the world forever.

"Are you sure you're all right?" It was the fourth time he'd asked me that question.

"Pretty sure," I said. But I really wasn't. It had been a terrifying experience, and my back hurt.

When I shivered, more from delayed reaction than from the cold, Jack took off his jacket and helped me slip it on.

"Why don't you keep it?" I said. "I'd rather feel the warmth of your arms than this jacket anyway."

"Don't worry about it." He put his arms back around me. "You can have both."

"But you'll be cold."

"Not likely. Right now I've got plenty of rage to keep me heated up." When he turned his head toward the sheriff's vehicle where Aaron had been cuffed and left in the back seat, even if I couldn't see Jack's face clearly in the dark, I knew there was fury bubbling up in him. I felt it in the tension of his body against my back.

It was comforting, in a way, to know he was angry that I'd been threatened and hurt, even if I didn't like seeing him stressed.

Sergeant Mackelroy came up, her stride and attitude bearing the weight of her authority. "You three can go inside and wait out of the cold," she said. "We'll be taking Mr. Bronson back to lockup, but Chief Deputy Boudreaux's on his way here. He's been briefed, and I'm sure he'll want formal statements from you, Miss Hamilton, and you, Mr. Fournet." I couldn't see the details of her face in the dark, but I had a feeling she was batting her lashes when she added, "And I know you'd like to get inside where it's nice and warm, Jack."

I tried not to pucker up and go all lemony, but I couldn't help it. "Yes, Jack, do come inside *with me* where it's nice and warm."

He took my hand. "Let's go then," he said. "You don't need to be out here any longer than necessary."

Jack and I started back toward the main building when I suddenly remembered... "Oh no, I forgot all about poor Stella. Jack, you gotta check on her."

But as it turned out, Stella was just fine. We met her as we walked up the steps to the veranda.

"Stella!" I said. "Oh, I'm so glad to see you. I was worried Zachary had gotten to you."

"He did, but it wasn't a bad thing after all. He was just worried about the fuzz coming around and wanted me to cast a chart to see if this was all going to turn out bad for him."

"So he wasn't on his way to beat you up?"

"Zachary? Beat *me* up? No, he'd never pull a downer like that on me. Don't know what I was thinking. I'm his meal ticket, you see."

I breathed a sigh of relief. She was all right. In fact, it was looking like almost everything was all right. Now, if they could just find out what Aaron did with Papa's bag.

Jack and I went to Jack's office. Odeo joined us. One of the kitchen staff brought hot cocoa at Jack's request, and we sat sipping it.

It was after twelve thirty in the morning when Harry Villars and Quincy walked in together.

Quincy frowned. "I knew you couldn't leave this alone," he scolded. "But then it looks like you may have caught one more dastardly killer. As a representative of the sheriff's office, I'd like to say thank you. As a friend, I'd like to ask you to stop putting yourself at risk like this. And as a man in love with special plans for the evening, I'd like to ask you if you couldn't have picked a more convenient time for me."

It was full-on Quincy at his most outrageous, and no comeback was required. I just took another sip from my mug of hot chocolate.

Harry looked pretty shaken up. I'd never seen him in such a state. Under his overcoat, his shirt had been buttoned up cockeyed, his slacks were beltless and wrinkled, and, holy smoke, the man wore no socks. Sleepy-eyed and messy-haired, it was my guess he'd been called out of a sound sleep at his New Orleans hotel when the alarm had gone off at his home, *la petite maison.*

Jack hurried to reassure him. "We're sort of back to normal here, Harry. At your place, it just turned out to be a few of the Ravens who set off the alarm by mistake. They were half-blind drunk, got turned around, and thought they were back at the resort by the patio doors to the Presto-Change-o Room. We found them sitting on the floor in the foyer, yelling for drink service."

Harry blinked a few times then ran his hand over his hair, smoothing it down a bit. "Well, can't blame a few guests for overindulging in holiday spirits. Can we?" But what seemed to really be on his mind was, "It truly was that young man, Aaron Bronson, who committed that heinous crime?"

"I'm afraid so," I said gently.

"And he tried to slay you as well, Miss Hamilton?" Disbelief and horror edged his voice.

I nodded, shivering with the memory of it. "But Odeo came to my rescue."

Harry clapped Odeo on the shoulder. "Thank the Lord for you, Odeo."

"Heck yeah," Jack said.

"Ditto," Quincy added.

I just smiled at Odeo, who'd ducked his head in kind of an *aw shucks* way at all the praise being heaped on him, and patted his hand.

Quincy pulled each of us aside and took our statements as to what had happened that night.

When we were done, he put away his notepad, stretched, and looked at his watch. "Woo-eee, after one already. Ferry quit running an hour ago, and Miss Cat probably gave up on me and hit the hay a long time ago anyway." He sighed and shook his head. "Not the evenin' I was hoping for. Didn't get to carry out my well-laid plan."

I didn't have any idea what he was talking about. "Well, you're gonna see her tomorrow anyway. You two are coming to my Grandmama Ida's tomorrow night after midnight mass, right?"

"Wouldn't miss it," he said. "But for now, I'm saying good night one and all. Looks like the murder of Papa Noël's been solved and put to bed." He winked at me. "We could call this one the mistletoe murder."

The adrenaline had long since worn off, and I started feeling pretty bad. My back still throbbed where I'd been hit with the shovel, and all my limbs had begun to ache. I hunched my shoulders and reached around to rub the sore spot on my back.

Jack reached for my hand. "Let's get you to the hospital."

I opened my mouth to object, but he didn't let me speak.

"Please, Mel, do it for me. Just to have you checked out."

"But I have two of the triplets to finish tomorrow morning."

"If the hospital clears you, I'll have you back here in plenty of time for them," Jack promised.

And he did get me back in time, but not plenty of time, not in my book anyway. There were no broken ribs or bruised lungs or kidneys, thank God, but it was still after four a.m. when he and I crawled into bed, curled up around each other, and went straight to sleep.

CHAPTER TWENTY-SEVEN

———

Getting out of bed Saturday morning, Christmas Eve day, was one of the most difficult physical challenges I'd ever faced. I lay on my back, Jack still cuddled up against me, his arm curled around me, holding me to him. His even breathing indicated he was still sleeping. I rolled one shoulder and let out a moan that woke him. He sat straight up.

"What is it?" His voice was husky with sleep, but the concern was unmistakable. "Are you all right?"

I moved my arm this time with the same result. "Ow." Somehow managing to roll onto my side, I slid my legs from under the covers, pulled myself into a sitting position, and set my feet on the floor. It took a lot of effort.

Turning around at Jack's sudden intake of breath, I caught him looking at my back in nothing short of horror.

"Oh, Mel. You're all black and blue and purple"—his voice sounded odd, husky and sad, and there was a catch that sounded almost like a shudder—"and green."

"Add gold, and I'd be a Mardi Gras float, f'sure," I said, trying to reassure him it wasn't as bad as it looked.

"I'm so sorry I wasn't there to keep this from happening." He swung out of bed, came to sit beside me, and wrapped his arms around me gently as if he feared I'd shatter into a thousand pieces. With his chin resting on top of my head, his jaw clenched, he gritted an oath so violent I cringed. I'd never heard anything like that from him before.

"Jack, how can you blame yourself? None of us knew it was Aaron," I said softly. "It's going to be okay. I'm sore, but nothing was broken. A little beaten up, but I'll be all right."

The tension in his body was contradicted by the tentative tenderness of his touch. "How about I go roust us out some breakfast?" He pulled back, and I looked up into his eyes that were suspiciously moist. "What sounds good?"

I smiled or tried to. Even that hurt. "Chicory coffee and toast with orange marmalade?"

He pursed his lips, thinking it over. "Strawberry jam?"

"Perfect," I said.

He kissed me on the lips, feather soft, and left me sitting on the bed.

While I watched him walk away toward the kitchen, it occurred to me that the man had an extremely fine bum for a Yankee—not that I hadn't noticed before. I also noticed how much his sweet concern had touched my heart.

* * *

The triplets showed up right on time at nine a.m. for their simians. The two remaining tattoos were Hear No Evil and Speak No Evil. There was an excellent lesson there for us all. A random thought made me ask myself why there was no fourth monkey sitting on his hands for Do No Evil.

The longer I worked, the looser I got, and by the time I finished, I wasn't half as sore as I'd been earlier. The triplets were pleased with my work, and I had to say they'd held up a lot better than the wimpy action star throughout the process. After signing a release form that allowed me to incorporate the mystic monkey designs into a portfolio, they took turns having their tatts photographed then paid me, tipped me nicely, checked out of the resort, and went on their merry way to spend the holiday with their mama.

"Our mama, she's just gonna go nuts 'bout these, " See No Evil said. "This way she'll know we've never forgotten all the good things she taught us."

I thought they were sweet men to think so highly of their mama.

Seeing as how it was Christmas Eve day, things had slowed down some at The Mansion, and the remaining two triplets had been my only appointments for the day. I closed up shop, hanging a sign on the door that said *Closed until Monday, December 26. Have a mystical Christmas.*

Cat's slate for the day was completely blank, and she hadn't even come in. I took the shuttle to the river to join her at our home sweet home in the Crescent City.

As I crossed on the Mystic Isle ferry that cold, windy day, watching the churning waters of the muddy Mississippi, it occurred to me that Cat might be grumpy because her plans with Quincy had been thwarted.

Cat and Quincy were such a great match—Q with his blunt, down-to-earth Cajun cockiness and occasionally off-kilter viewpoint and Cat with more than enough backbone and common sense to keep him grounded. And they were both so good-looking if they ever did tie the knot and start a family, the children would be stunning. How come that man hadn't bought her a ring and dropped a knee yet? He'd better get on with it pretty soon. Cat was the kind of gal who'd take the matter into her own hands, and if he wasn't ready to commit by the time she was, that woman would move on to greener pastures. Didn't that fool of a man know he'd found his soul mate?

And speaking of soul mates, I was beginning to think I might have found mine. The way Jack's eyes had clouded that morning when he saw the bruises on my back, the way his hands had been so achingly tender and gentle when he'd touched me, and the way he'd insisted on propping me up in bed then bringing a tray with toast, strawberry jam, and the perfect cup of chicory and coffee fixed up *regulah*, just the way I liked it—it all came back to me, and my throat tightened with emotion. Did I love him? Yes. Did I love him enough for a lifetime? Maybe. Did he love me? I thought that yes, it was likely he did. And that gave me comfort and warmth as I snuggled into my winter jacket against the cold wind and watched the ferry pilot, my friend George, tie up to the dock on the city side of the river.

I walked the few blocks to home where Cat had a cheery fire burning in the fireplace.

When I walked in she looked up from the table where she was wrapping holiday packages. "I checked the newspaper, and Gypsy Lady didn't come in for us."

"Huh?" It took me a minute to catch up. "Oh, the horse. The bet. Well, there ya are. So much for an illustrious career as professional gamblers."

"Yeah." She snipped the end off a ribbon and set one pretty package aside before starting on the next. "That's what I figured too."

I ran a hot bath and soaked my aching bones in our big ol' claw-foot tub, not climbing out until the water began to cool.

From the great room, the sound of Cat singing Christmas carols off-key rang out as she strung boxes, bags, ribbons, and paper across the dining room table, wrapping all the bounty we'd gathered up haunting the excellent secondhand shops and boutiques.

Except for the gifts for our men, which were as individual as those two guys were, we'd pooled our money for gift giving. Both our names would go on all the gift tags, and there was something on our table we'd handpicked for almost everyone we knew.

CHAPTER TWENTY-EIGHT

———

Jack and Quincy had crossed the river and came by at four to pick us up in Quincy's Ford Explorer. All four of us headed out to the hospital and joined Father Brian who showed us to the sterile isolation ward where Nicole had been housed.

She'd been admitted to the sterile environment prior to her bone marrow transplant scheduled to take place on Christmas Day because the donor had to leave for a church mission in Africa as soon as she'd been cleared to travel.

We couldn't speak to Nicole, but all five of us stood in the hallway outside the big pane-glass window and waved. She looked wan and tired with big dark circles against the creamy skin under her dark eyes. She wore a blue chemo skullcap patterned with Olaf, the snowman from *Frozen*. When she smiled, it was hard not to notice her grey lips and the effort it took for her to raise her arm and wave back. To me, it was one of the great mysteries of life why little children had to suffer.

After Aaron had been taken to lockup, a search of his apartment had indeed turned up the bag taken from Papa Noël. All but $5,000 of the cash was gone from it. Aaron not only admitted the murder, but also that the money had been sent for Benjy's tuition.

The music school turned the money straight over to the Jefferson Parish sheriff who'd seen that it was released back to St. Antoine's Children's Home within hours. That huge chunk of money along with additional donations from the generous parishioners at the church came just in time to facilitate the medical procedure.

Father Brian bowed his head, placing his hand on the plate glass between the girl and us. Cat and I did the same, nudging Quincy and Jack when Father Brian began to speak. Their chins lowered too.

"Our Lord and God, please watch over this sweet child tomorrow. Guide her doctors' hands, and give her a healing treatment and full recovery."

Cat, Quincy, and I said, "Amen."

Jack's *Amen* came a beat later, and his voice broke then he helped me back on with my fancy full-length black wool coat—the one I only wore on special occasions like Christmas Eve midnight mass and New Year's Eve at Thibadeaux's Bar in the French Quarter.

Father Brian turned to us. "I'll see you all later at services?"

"Yes, Father," I said. "You will."

We made our way back out to the parking lot. It was Jack's first N'awlins Christmas, and I absolutely wanted him to drink it all in, so we'd planned a night of streetcar riding to all the brightly decorated neighborhoods: Canal Street, the Garden District, and the Quarter. We even stopped to take a stroll at City Park through Celebration of the Oaks.

I loved my city. Couldn't imagine living anywhere else, and sharing its holiday beauty with Jack was so special.

Tonight was also special because it was the first Christmas midnight mass that had been celebrated at St. Antoine's Parish in the Ninth Ward since Katrina had all but obliterated the beautiful old church. The loyal parishioners, me included, and even a time or two my Cap'n Jack, had donated time, spare change, and energy to her restoration. After so many years, the building had been restored and was beautiful for the special service.

The building was filled to the brim. Candles flickered along the walls and in the sanctuary.

The four of us took seats about halfway back in the nave.

Jack leaned over and asked me, "You think this might be one of the pews I painted last summer?"

I took a good look at it and couldn't tell, but I still patted his hand and said, "It does sort of look like one of those you worked on."

The choir sounded like angels, singing some of the more religious Christmas carols, as the altar boys and Father Brian proceeded up the aisle to the altar.

The choir ended their song. Father Brian approached the podium, held up his hands in welcome, and said, "Let us pray."

We bowed our heads and followed his lead.

After the service was over, we left the building into the cold, starless night. The wind had died, and at the late hour, the streets were quiet as we drove to Grandmama Ida's house in the Holy Cross neighborhood for a traditional réveillon dinner.

My mama and grandmama and quite a few of their friends gathered on Christmas Eve day to cook and bake and pile up enough food to feed the New Orleans Saints front line, back line, coaches, cheerleaders, and all supporting staff. Even Ruby, the owner of Ruby's Famous Bourbon Chicken where Mama had worked as manager for as long as I could remember, usually showed up with two stainless steel chafing dishes, one with her awesome specialty chicken and the other with beans and dirty rice.

Grandmama Ida's place, a shotgun-style duplex where my mama lived in one half and Grandmama the other, was strung all around with Christmas lights. A lighted nativity scene with lots of real hay and old-fashioned (and maybe a little cheesy) figurines decorated the front lawn. Big old Styrofoam candy canes wound with red and white LED lights lined the front porch. Inside, the whole house looked like Christmas and smelled like heaven.

"Holy smoke," Jack said. "Just standing here, my mouth's watering."

When dinner was served, we all made right fools of ourselves, eating and drinking and talking and laughing until the wee hours of the morning.

Jack, Quincy, Cat, and my mama gathered on Grandmama's tired, saggy old sofa to look at an old photo album with pictures of my family all the way back to the post-Civil War days.

I took the time to walk out onto the front porch where it was quiet and calm, and the twinkling candy canes, the plastic Joseph, Mary, and Jesus were the only lights.

I'd wrapped my arms around myself and stood looking up at the sky when Grandmama Ida walked up behind me and wrapped her arms around me too. "What's troubling you, baby?" she asked.

I gave a little laugh. "Never can hide anything from you. Can I?"

"Course not." She chuckled. "Why bother even trying?"

So I began, first telling her about the dream I'd had and then about what had happened at the cemetery.

She stood there looking out on the street where lights were still on in most of the neighboring houses at that early-morning hour as others held their own réveillon. When I was about halfway done with the telling, she took hold of my hand and brought me down with her to sit on the top step on the stoop.

When I finished I said, "I know we've talked about this before, but it's happening more often now, and I'm not sure what I should do about it."

She didn't say anything for a while, but I could tell she was thinking about what I'd said by the way she was sucking her teeth.

"Why do you think something ought to be done about it, child?" she finally asked. "And just what are you thinking that something might be?"

I shrugged. "I don't know. I just don't understand it, I guess."

"It's not for you to understand," she said. "Your granddaddy, he loved you more than his very own life. And if he's watching over you, why, missy, there's nothing for you to do except listen to the advice that old man gives you—it's gonna be solid gold—and maybe every once in a while just say, 'Thank you, Granddaddy Joe.'"

I sighed and leaned over and kissed her plump cheek. She shooed me away like I was a gnat buzzing her head, but I knew she treasured that kiss just like she treasured me.

There wasn't even a whisper of wind, not that I'd noticed anyway, yet for some reason, Granddaddy's old rocker began to move by itself, creaking back and forth just like in the old days when he'd sat in it morning, noon, and night.

Grandmama Ida and I turned to stare at it. When it didn't stop, she looked back at me and winked.

I winked back and said, "Thank you, Granddaddy Joe."

CHAPTER TWENTY-NINE

———

Cat and I both slept in past ten then we got up and made our rounds to family and friends, dropping off all the treasures we'd so patiently shopped for nearly all year long.

It was Sunday afternoon as we rode across the river. Christmas Day, after the longest two days of my life, or it had seemed so—from the time I'd gotten out of bed and Cat and I had made our first foray into the realm of illegal betting on Friday morning until the early morning hours of Christmas Eve and the réveillon dinner at Grandmama Ida's with its eye-opening realization of the guardian angel watching over me, my granddaddy, Joe.

I carried my portfolio with me. Its contents were something special I had for Cap'n Jack.

Cat's phone rang just before we docked. It was "Cornbread," a really popular Zydeco song, and that meant Quincy was calling.

She put the phone to her ear and made the connection. "Why if it isn't that world famous lawman Quincy Boudreaux."

I listened while Cat made mostly monosyllabic replies. "Yes—sure—oh, great—right—not at all. Thanks for letting us know, my Cajun lover. You're the best."

She disconnected and faced me.

"Feel like sharing?" I asked.

"That was my man. He was calling to tell me that Aaron had made a full confession, even copping to that string of thefts at The Mansion. It was all for Valentine, all to get money for Benjy's tuition."

I had begun to suspect as much. "And he killed Slim because he thought their fabricated affair sullied Valentine's reputation?"

Cat shook her head as if she couldn't believe the scope of Aaron's terrible deeds. "And once he discovered the cash in the goodie bag, Aaron could stop robbing the resort guests and just anonymously hand it all over to the Childress Music Academy. Q said Aaron justified it all by having made a promise to Tyrell Cantrell."

"Unbelievable," I said.

"The sheriffs spent yesterday taking inventory of the Christmas goodie bag they found in Aaron's apartment, and then the sheriff requested a special circumstance dispensation from the court so he could return the bag to Harry Villars."

"So that's how Harry was able to set up tonight's party for the kids."

"That's how," she said.

There was one other thing that had been bothering me. "Did Quincy have any news about Odeo? There was talk he might be charged with some kind of complicity because he knew about Slim selling liquor out of the boathouse."

She shook her head. "Harry had a talk with Odeo. In all the years Odeo's worked for Harry, there hasn't been a single problem. Harry scolded Odeo for not coming to him when he learned what Slim was doing, but at the same time, he convinced the police not to charge Odeo with anything. Odeo's all good now."

I breathed a sigh of relief. "I'm glad of that. He saved my life, and I'd feel pretty low if anything bad happened to him."

We docked and disembarked with the few others who'd crossed.

The Mansion at Mystic Isle shuttle waited at the end of the walkway. I didn't recognize today's driver. He might have been someone new unlucky enough to get stuck working on Christmas Day. I reached in my bag for one of the small sacks of Christmas cookies Mama and Grandmama Ida had baked yesterday.

"Merry Christmas," I held the cookies out.

He took them and smiled. "Thank you. And you have yourself a good one too."

Cat and I found a couple of seats and rode on over to The Mansion while a Michael Bublé holiday CD played over the speakers.

The Mystic Mistletoe Merriment Rehash Bash was set for six p.m. Before I went to the resort dining room where the party was being held, I headed to Jack's place. He opened the door, seeming surprised to see me as if I'd interrupted him, but then he took me in his arms and kissed me soundly.

"Merry Christmas, Miss Hamilton."

I pulled away, walked in, opened my portfolio, and pulled out the canvas. "Merry Christmas, Mr. Stockton," I said, handing him the 15x19 inch frame with a big silver bow around it.

He looked at me quizzically before turning it around. I crossed my fingers behind my back then uncrossed them, my heart quivering at the look of awe and appreciation on his face.

He shifted the canvas to one hand, reached for me, and drew me into his arms. "It's me," he said simply. "I love it."

It was, indeed, my Cap'n Jack in his best navy blue suit, wearing his resort name tag, standing arms akimbo in front of The Mansion. It took me weeks to finish it. I'd originally thought to paint him in swashbuckling pirate garb, the way I always thought of him. But then he'd probably have hung it somewhere discreet and couldn't show it off to others.

His smiling eyes looked away from mine back to the painting. He left me to set it on a chair and then stood back, looking at it.

"How did you…when did you…aw, Mel, it's just great."

I was warm all over. He loved it. I'd hoped he would but wasn't sure. "I worked on it on my days off when I took my other stuff to Jackson Square to sell. Everyone seemed to like it. Some folks even stopped and asked if they could buy it. " I ducked my head, suddenly shy. "They said it made them feel good, happy, like a lot of love had been put in it."

"Love?" He caught his breath. "I have something for you too." He left the room, returning quickly with a small red gift bag.

Suddenly excited, I grinned up at him and opened it, pulling out the tissue paper to reveal the teeniest, tiniest of black bikinis. I held it up. "Oh my." Then I looked at him.

He stood grinning at me. "You like it?"

"Sure," I said. "But, Jack, it's December. It's cold outside."

"Keep looking," he said patiently.

I reached into the bag again. There was an envelope, which I took out and opened.

"It's not cold in Florida," Jack said.

I gasped. "Really? We're going to Florida?" It was a printed airline ticket confirmation for two roundtrip tickets to Palm Beach. I threw myself at him. "I can't wait."

"Neither can I," he said. "My parents live in Palm Beach. I want them to meet the woman who's stolen my heart."

I stopped and stood back, startled.

"What's wrong?" he asked, frowning. "Don't you want to meet my mom and dad?"

"Yes." My voice was shaky. "But what if they don't like me?"

"Like you? They'll love you." He paused. "Just like I do."

CHAPTER THIRTY

————

There weren't as many people present at this Christmas party as on the night of that first fateful event, nor was the place quite as spiffed up.

Valentine's staff hadn't been able to prepare nearly as elaborate a menu, but the holiday buffet they had come up with looked and tasted delish. The buffet had been served. We all were full to the brim when Jack excused himself after the meal to take care of some detail he'd forgotten. I missed him already.

The one aspect of the party that exceeded the first was Lurch and Marvin's rendition of "Jingle Bell Rock." They sang in harmony. Lurch's voice so low it kind of rumbled the room, but it was pretty terrific. And I was kind of getting used to the way they both looked in the elf costumes.

When they finished, the double doors burst open and Papa Noël bounded into the room. But who was it behind that beard? After what happened to Slim, no one wanted to be Papa Noël—unless you counted Marvin. I'd heard that both Harry and Jack thanked him but said they had someone else in mind who'd agreed to do it.

Cat and Quincy were kind of cuddled together, she leaning into him. At Papa Noël's energetic entrance, Cat said, "That's some way good action for an old fat Christmas sprite."

"It is that," Quincy added. "Who'd they con into playing the old boy, anyway?"

I shrugged. I hadn't been included in Jack and Harry's final plan, so I was as much in the dark as any of them.

He was a good-looking Papa Noël all right, straight-backed and strong with the heavy bag on one shoulder. He treated the room to a resounding, "Ho, ho, ho, y'all. Yat?"

I sat up straight. Jack. It was Jack. I covered my mouth with one hand to keep myself from blurting out his name as he went straight to the big old throne covered in red velvet that had been pulled from one of the magic-show venues on the property. He plopped down into the chair.

His accent was just pitiful, but I loved him for every drawled out word.

"I am so sorry about not getting here earlier, boys and girls, but those old gators of mine." He took a sheet of paper from inside one of the fur-lined sleeves and read, " Gaston, Tiboy, Pierre, Alcee, Ninette, Suzette, Celeste, and Renee were acting up." His accent slipped away, and he mispronounced a couple of the gators' names, but he was still just about the best Papa Noël I'd ever seen—at least the sexiest.

The children all gathered around, and there was a present for each and every one of them.

Harry Villars took over the mic on the dais at one end of the room. "You've probably all noticed our sweet girl, Nicole, isn't present with us on this lovely occasion. And that's because her bone marrow transplant was today. Her Christmas gift will be a new lease on life. Now, what do you lovely people think 'bout that?"

Cheers and applause broke out. I looked around the table at my friends: Cat, Quincy, Fabrizio, Stella, and Valentine. From across the table, Cat gave me a thumbs up, but Valentine seemed lost in thought.

I reached over and took hold of her hand. "A penny for 'em," I said.

"For my thoughts?" she asked.

She smiled a little. Melancholy was what I would have called her mood. And why not? None of this had turned out all that great for her. The tragic death of her husband had basically been revealed to be the cause of a friend dying, another friend going to prison, and the recovery of Papa's loot had turned out to result in the defunding of her son's musical education. She had good reason to be quiet and reflective.

I nodded.

She began. "I was just wondering if maybe I'd been wrong to try and help poor Slim with his stressful issues. I mean, it was the start of the bad times, after all. Slim's gone. Aaron, as wrong as he was, is going to spend the rest of his life behind bars when all he was doing was trying to live up to some sad notion he owed it to Tyrell to watch over me."

I shook my head. "No, Valentine. It wasn't you. None of it. It was all Aaron." I couldn't help asking about the other reason I figured she was sad that night. "And now Benjy can't go to the academy either."

"Oh, no, child." It always sort of bothered me when Valentine called me that. As wise and motherly as she was, she was only eight years older than I was. "Benjy, he'll be going to Childress all right. When the money Aaron sent in was confiscated by the sheriff"—she glanced over at Quincy—"or rather the sheriff's chief deputy"—Quincy had the grace for once to duck his head—"the dean of Childress went to the board and arranged a full scholarship for my boy." She smiled, and it was genuine. "You better ask for that child's autograph now, while his head's not all swollen up."

I laughed.

Her expression sobered. "Mel, have you heard anything about that Connor woman?"

"She spent a couple of nights in the hospital." Quincy joined the conversation. "Temporary psychosis. Dat's what they saying. If she agrees to treatment, the judge, he tell her he's maybe going to commute her sentence from kidnapping to child endangerment."

I looked at Valentine to see how she felt about that. "Poor, sad woman," was all she said.

"Poor, sad woman? I don't think so," Quincy said. "She a nut job."

I pretty much agreed with him.

All the ceremonies were over with by now, and my Cap'n Jack, who'd turned out to be a truly awesome Papa Noël, was headed to our table.

He leaned over, pulled down his beard, and surprised me with a warm, lustful kiss on the lips.

"Well, now," Stella said. "You got one for an old flower child too, Papa?"

Jack's belly laugh was so long and deep all his padding seemed to shift sideways a little. "Why, no, Madam Stella, I don't." He circled around the table to Cat and Quincy. "But I do have a little something else I was asked to bring with me tonight."

He set a small Christmas gift bag in front of Quincy, leaned over, and said softly, "Good luck, bro," before looking up at me, winking, and then leaving the room with another loud, "Ho, ho, ho. Merry Christmas to all, and to all a good night, y'all."

I just loved that man.

Every eye at the table was locked onto that pretty little red Christmas bag in front of Quincy.

"What's that?" Cat asked.

Quincy leaned in and draped his arm across her shoulders. "Now, now, chère, don't you be knowing what curiosity did to the *Cat*?"

We all turned around as Harry's voice, slow and slightly lazy from all the holiday spirits, came over the mic. "We're going to have a little Zydeco Christmas music from The Ragtime Players, featuring the man with that special touch, Mr. Desi Lopez de Monterra. So by all means, friends, let's dance the night away."

Harry moved off the dais as several men hustled around setting up the instruments for the band.

There was going to be music. Dancing.

I wanted to dance and wished Jack was here, and then he was, looking just like a Hollywood hunk on Oscar night in his tux. He was suddenly behind my chair. Just magical, but then wasn't magic the norm at The Mansion on Mystic Isle?

"Didn't expect to see you for a little while yet," I looked up at him.

He grinned down at me. "I wouldn't have missed this for the world."

I frowned. "Missed what?"

Jack looked across the table, so I did too.

Quincy shoved back his chair, slipped out of it, and dropped to one knee. I thought I saw his hand shaking as he reached for the bag, took out a small velvet box, and flipped it open. The light hit the diamond, and all of us took in a breath that sounded like a collective sigh.

"Catalina Gabor, love of my life, goddess divine, will you grant me the extreme honor of becoming my wife?"

There was a long pause. Too long for us to all be sure what the answer was going to be, and as thrilled as I was, a moment of doubt waffled through me.

But then, the answer came, and just as I'd known she would, my friend threw her arms around her handsome, crazy Cajun man, nearly knocking him over, and said, "Well, it's about darn time, Chief Deputy. Now put that big sparkler on my finger and kiss me."

What a sweet, beautiful moment. Sentimental tears moistened my eyes.

I looked back up at Jack. He was looking back at me, his gaze intense, riveting, and I couldn't look away. His beautiful, cinnamon-colored eyes never leaving mine, he leaned down and whispered in my ear, "Give you any ideas, Miss Hamilton?"

Caught by surprise, I had nothing to say except, "Oh, Cap'n Jack."

And from somewhere out in the cosmos, I was pretty sure there was laughter—laughter that sounded an awful lot like Granddaddy Joe.

In case you're thinking of having your own holiday party, why not mix up a few of these potent babies. Of course, if you follow the recipe, your guests will be less likely to fall off their stools than Mel's were.

Hurricane, New Orleans Style Recipe

1 oz white rum
1 oz Jamaican dark rum
1 oz Bacardi 151 rum
3 oz orange juice
3 oz unsweetened pineapple juice
1/2 oz grenadine syrup
crushed ice

Combine all ingredients, mix well (shake or stir). Pour over crushed ice in hurricane glass. Best enjoyed through a small straw and in a beautiful hurricane glass while listening to Dixieland jazz (in New Orleans if at all possible). Garnish with fruit wedge (or two or three) if desired. Sit back with your hurricane, and wait till it all blows over.

ABOUT THE AUTHORS

USA Today bestselling authors Sally J. Smith and Jean Steffens are partners in crime—crime writing, that is. They live in Scottsdale, Arizona, awesome for eight months out of the year, an inferno the other four. They write bloody murder, flirty romance, and wicked humor all in one package. When their heads aren't together over a manuscript, you'll probably find them at a movie or play, a hockey game or the mall, or at one of the hundreds of places to find a great meal in the Valley of the Sun.

To learn more about Sally J. Smith and Jean Steffens, visit them online at: www.smithandsteffens.com

Enjoyed this book? Check out these other reads available in print now from Gemma Halliday Publishing:

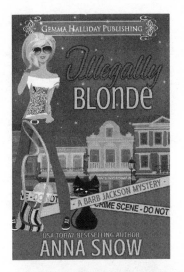

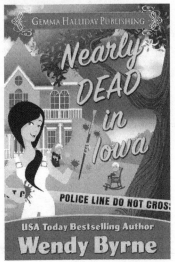

Made in the USA
San Bernardino, CA
28 November 2016